MADMAN ON MAIN STREET

by Elaine A. Kule

1

I, Michael Dane, age 12, am not the world's best student. I'm not even Centerville Junior High's best student. Far from it. Okay, I don't try all that hard. What I have, according to my teachers, is potential. But if I hear "You don't make the slightest effort to reach your maximum potential" once more, I'm going to scream. Which is what my parents did when they saw my last report card.

You're probably thinking I should just do the work so everyone will quit nagging me. But here's the way I see it: Books will always be around. So will math, science, and history. On the other hand, playing JV basketball, or watching a really great game on TV, well, this stuff *won't* keep. Last Friday, though, Coach Nelson said that my grades have to improve or I'll get thrown off the team. And I wouldn't be surprised if my folks made me give up TV for the next 30 years.

One thing I'll never give up is my paper route. It's my only source of income. Dad's always saying, "There's no such thing as a free lunch in this world. You want something, you have to earn it." Well, I want—no, make that need—baseball cards, a small amount of junk food (my mother won't buy it), and other essentials too numerous to mention. So, I'm up before dawn every day, making sure the good citizens of Centerville—those on my route, that is—have the news to digest with their breakfasts.

Yesterday morning I noticed another customer on my distribution list: Abner Hilks. I'd never heard that name before, but the address, 200 Main Street, sounded familiar. Could it be the spooky old place that's been deserted ever since I can remember? Nah. Who'd want to live there?

I hopped on my bike and began my rounds.

FRIGHT TIME

3 Spine-tingling Tales
for Young Readers

- MADMAN ON MAIN STREET
- SCARY HARRY
- IT'S ALMOST DARK

BARONET

Baronet Books, New York, New York

MADMAN ON MAIN STREET

But as I neared the last stop, my heart sank a bit. There it was, the old sorry-looking house. Whatever paint there was had chipped and faded. The front yard had weeds a foot high. This place, sitting at the end of Main Street, was the one kids used to think was haunted. Me included. It got so bad that Billy Smith's father once took a bunch of us inside to explore the place, just to prove we were wrong. Nothing happened, but even so I walked home unconvinced. I mean, no ghost or goblin would pull a stunt in broad daylight. Not with Mr. Smith around. The man is almost seven feet tall. He's a great guy and everything, but you don't mess with Billy's dad. Even if you're an evil spirit.

I'm not saying I believe in haunted houses. Still, as I got to 200 Main, I had a rolled newspaper in my hand, ready to throw on the rickety front porch. But I stopped mid-toss. Sitting in a weather-beaten rocking chair was a gray-haired man with a longish beard. No introductions were necessary. This had to be Abner Hilks.

"Good morning, Michael," he said.

I froze. It wasn't so much that he knew my name; the newspaper's subscription department could have told him. What got me was his voice.

FRIGHT TIME

It was the creepiest thing I'd ever heard, so scary it gave me chills. Trust me, I've seen tons of horror movies, but just the sound of this guy beat them all. Besides, seeing a movie is one thing. Being so close to the real thing is another. I decided that I'd better shove off. But Abner's next comment had me glued to the spot.

"Having trouble in school, eh? A shame. Knowledge is power. Don't you forget it."

I was too stunned to talk. How could he possibly know about my low grades? Just when I calmed down enough to ask him, Abner got up from the chair, opened the front door, and went inside. He was holding a rolled newspaper. I suddenly realized that I had never given him one. I peddled to school as fast as I could. For the first time in a long time, I was glad to get there.

But the rest of the day grew even stranger.

For starters, math was a disaster. Ms. Reynolds made a sarcastic comment after I told her that I'd forgotten my homework—again. Some of the kids laughed. I really hate that. First of all, I don't think teachers should embarrass a kid in front of everyone. And if that sort of thing does happen, I think the class should stick together; in other words, don't make the kid feel worse. To tell you the truth, I've never laughed when, say, Coach Nelson yells at someone for missing a clear shot—during practice, no less. Then, in history, Mr. Benton gave a pop quiz. It was on the chapter he asked us to read last night. Trouble is, I'd left the textbook in my locker. I guess I didn't feel like lugging the thing home just to read a few pages. I also figured I should wait until I was more in the mood. Obviously, I thought wrong. And wouldn't you know, the quiz was the essay type. No assist with some lucky multiple-choice guesswork.

I really sweated the first question. It's hard to pretend you know stuff when you really don't. And besides, trying to fool Mr. Benton is ridiculous. When it comes to history, the man is a walking encyclopedia.

The second question was really tough. While imagining how I could try to sound halfway intelligent, my eyes wandered toward the hallway. I saw a shadowy figure lurking in a dark corner. I felt my heart sink when I realized it was Abner Hilks. He just stood there, staring at me with a weird grin. What was he doing here? I shuddered. The guy gave me the creeps, that's for sure.

Maybe it was all that stress in one day, but I

actually thought the classroom walls were closing in on me. I had to leave, to breathe fresh air. But Abner was out there. Who was he waiting for? I'll be honest: I was more afraid of him than some old test score. Since I couldn't think any more anyway, I handed in an almost blank paper. I walked back to my desk, folded my arms, and rested my aching head on them.

Minutes later, I thought I was hearing things when Mr. Benton praised me for a perfect grade. I was so flabbergasted I nearly fell off my chair. Then, for some reason, I glanced at the corridor again. It was deserted. I felt relieved—until I heard the echo of a weird chuckle. Abner, no doubt. I couldn't help thinking that he had something to do with changing the exam I gave my teacher. But how? And why?

Fortunately, the bell rang and my thoughts were interrupted by versions of "Good going, Michael." I also got a few nods and smiles from kids who never looked at me before—namely Tracy Scott, the most popular girl in our grade. I have to admit, it all felt pretty good—better than being laughed at anyway. At least I managed to get my mind off Abner Hilks.

But not for long.

2

I don't really have a best friend, not since Larry Andrews moved away last year. Between my job, school, and JV, I'm busy enough. And I get along really well with the guys on the team. But no one's like Larry. He's the brother I never had—a true bud. We take turns phoning one another, just as we promised, but it's not the same. I mean, the guy had lived next door.

The people who moved into Larry's house are okay, although I'm not that crazy about Cara. She's this 11-year-old and a bit of a know-it-all. I'm sure you know the type; they're everywhere. Very annoying. Anyway, just when I rode up my driveway, Cara popped out of her door, as if she were waiting for me.

"Can I ask you a question?"

"You just did." I quickly stored my bike in the garage, hoping for a fast getaway. If there was one thing I'd had my fill of, it was answering questions. And Cara picked the wrong time to say anything beyond our usual hi.

"C'mon."

"Oh, go ahead, but make it fast." My favorite

9

TV show would be on any minute, but I wasn't about to tell her that.

"Well, a few kids said there was a haunted house around here. I thought they were teasing, but they looked serious."

"Do you really think there's such a thing as a haunted house?" I was practically barking at the kid, but her timing was awful. Floating in my head were snapshots of Abner—on the porch, in the hallway. I had to get rid of them, and Cara.

"What's the matter with you? You look like you've seen a ghost."

That did it. "I'm tired, I'm starving. Stop worrying about all this crazy stuff and go do your homework or something."

Just then Mom poked her head out the door. "Come inside, you two. I just made some cocoa."

Cara smiled at me, as if to apologize. "I'm staying at your house this afternoon. My mother had to take Beth to the doctor." Beth is Cara's four-year-old sister.

I was mad, but this was one of those times when you just can't show it. Which, if you ask me, is very difficult. But of all days to be stuck with Cara! I really needed to zone out for a while and watch TV. Now, for Mom's sake, I'd have to be polite to someone who was really getting on my nerves.

The cocoa was too hot to gulp. I thought about bringing it to my room, but I knew Mom would never allow that sort of thing. (I could hear her saying that she won't tolerate rudeness to a guest. And I can hear myself replying that I didn't invite her. Good thing this conversation is imaginary.)

So I sat there, listening to Cara drone on about her latest round of A's and Excellent's. I'll admit she works very hard. In fact, I'll bet all she does is study. Anyway, just when I thought the kid was running out of steam, I noticed her staring at the history paper I'd stuffed into my notebook.

"Here I am talking about myself and you got an A-plus."

Mom, rinsing a pot at the sink, turned around. "Michael, that's wonderful. Why didn't you say anything?"

Because I didn't do anything, I thought. How could I ever explain what happened? Even if I had read the assigned chapter, would I have done so well? Not a chance. Now she'd expect more of the same—which I could never deliver. I was furious at Cara for being such a blabbermouth. And I wanted to kick myself for not doing a better job of hiding the stupid paper. I wasn't ready to destroy it yet; first I wanted to read the test answers—behind closed doors!

Mom was standing over me, beaming, her hand extended a bit for the paper. As I pulled the page from my notebook, I saw something scribbled in an unfamiliar—strange, actually—handwriting. I didn't have time to read it with Mom waiting, but right after commenting on the grade, her eyes zeroed in.

"'Knowledge is power. A.H.' I agree. Who's A.H.?"

I mumbled that he was someone new in school. Not entirely untrue.

Cara—Miss Nosy—was peering at the message. "What kind of handwriting is that? It looks like something from the Middle Ages."

"It's a joke. Can't you tell it's a joke?" I got the paper back from Mom, raced upstairs to my room, and closed the door. I caught a glimpse of myself in the mirror above the bureau. Cara was right. I did look scared. Probably because I was.

I sat on my bed, relieved to be alone in my room. I glanced around, thinking that although the room was the same since I'd left it, I felt different. I'd had the most bizarre day ever of experiencing things that I didn't understand and couldn't control. And there was no one to help me.

A knock on my door made me jump. I was Mom.

"Are you okay, Michael?"

"Sure, Mom. I'm just really tired. Think I'll lie down for a while."

"All right. Let me know if you need anything."

"Thanks." It's amazing what a top-notch grade will buy. Mom doesn't usually let me get off that easily.

It was true, though. I was exhausted. I must have fallen asleep within minutes. When I awoke, it was dark. I looked at the clock on my night table. Three a.m.! I wondered if I could enter myself in the Guinness Book of Records.

I was starving. After freshening up quietly, so as not to wake anyone, I fixed myself a huge bowl of milk and cereal. Then, instead of hanging around, I decided to get dressed and begin my route a little earlier than usual. It wasn't because I'd grown so ambitious. I just figured that maybe I'd avoid seeing Abner.

I was the first kid at the distribution center that morning, and even though it was out of my way, I made a beeline for 200 Main Street. No sign of Abner. I quickly aimed a newspaper in the general direction of his porch, without bothering to check where it landed. I let out a deep breath and smiled at my cleverness. Today was going to be a good day, I just knew it.

I jammed on my brakes when I realized one important thing: I'd fallen asleep last night before doing my homework. Panic set in. There was that short essay to complete for English, 10 math problems, and an outline for the project I was doing for the science fair—which I haven't even thought about yet. And I couldn't dash anything off now, not with a load of papers I still had to deliver.

Ms. Franklin, my English teacher, isn't big on formalities. She just has kids drop off their work in a basket that sits on her desk. I felt like a jerk this morning, acting busy while everyone else had something to hand in. Finally, I couldn't stand it any more. I had to confess. I approached Ms. Franklin and told her I'd been too ill to write the essay. Another half-truth.

"I don't understand," she said, looking at the pile. "Your work is right on top."

I couldn't believe it. There, in my own handwriting, was a fine-looking composition. I could feel my face turning bright red, especially since Ms. Franklin was eyeing me with a puzzled expression. "Michael, is there something wrong? Something you'd like to tell me?"

I walked backward to my desk, hoping some distance would save me. "Uh, no. No, I'm fine, really. Guess I forgot that I didn't forget. To do the assignment, I mean. Before I got sick."

Luckily, no one seemed to be hearing any of my babbling. Still, I felt stupid and confused, too dazed to figure any of it out.

And it didn't end there. My math homework had been completed. So was the science project outline. As I rode home on my bicycle after JV practice, I started wondering if maybe some guardian angel was helping me. And why not? When you stop to think about it, I *am* a pretty decent kid. . . . Michael, I thought, get a grip.

At this hour I usually take the shortcut, even though it means riding along a deserted path. My parents don't know, but then again, it has never come up. I always crank up the pace, because as soon as the sun goes down, the place gets a little spooky.

I saw some sort of rag caught in the front

wheel. I braked and stooped over to remove the thing. Then, out of the corner of my eye, I saw something move from behind a tree. My heart pounded wildly when I saw who it was.

"Sorry I missed seeing you this morning. But homework assignments require sufficient time, even for me. In any case, I hope they'll be received well by your teachers."

There's no point denying I was frightened, but I couldn't let Abner see that. Putting on the stern face I've seen a million times on my father and Coach Nelson, I looked the old man in the eye. "Who are you and what do you want? Why are you doing my work? Of all the kids in Centerville, why me?"

The man chuckled—the same awful sound I'd heard in the corridor. It gave me the shivers.

"I suppose we haven't been formally introduced. But as you are probably aware, I'm Abner Hilks. That answers your first question. As to what I want, you'll be told in good time, boy. All in good time."

He vanished. So did my false bravery. I was shaking so hard I could barely climb on my bike. As I pedaled home, Abner's crazed laughter kept playing in my head, over and over again.

3

I was panting so hard by the time I got home that it brought Cara to her bedroom window. "Keep it down, will you? I'm trying to study. Gee, Michael, you sound just like an old man."

You would, too, I thought, if you'd just beaten the all-time record for Bike Racing After Seeing a Weirdo. Hearing her complain like that made me think of Larry again. I needed to talk to him, especially about all that was happening. Our parents said we could phone each other whenever we wanted—within reason, of course. There wasn't a better reason than now.

He answered on the first ring. I felt instantly better after hearing his hello.

"Larry, hi, it's me."

"Mikey, how ya doin'?"

"Okay, I guess. You?"

"So-so. School's a drag, just like in Centerville. What's going on?"

"Not much." My usual reply came automatically. "Scratch that. Plenty. How much time have you got?"

"All you need. Shoot."

17

FRIGHT TIME

That's Larry for you. Always there when you need him, even when he's not there. I told him about Abner and the loony things that had been happening. He didn't doubt a word. That's Larry for you.

"So, what do you think?" I asked.

"I think you'd better be careful. This guy sounds nuts. Maybe you should consider another line of work."

"You're forgetting this is Centerville. And that I'm 12 years old. There are child labor laws, you know."

"You could try baby-sitting."

That cracked us both up. The one and only time I baby-sat—two years ago—was for the Jenkins boys. These kids, ages three and five, nearly tore their house apart and were gunning for me next. I had quickly phoned Larry to bail me out. He came over right away and got the boys involved in a video while I cleaned up. By the time Mrs. Jenkins got home from the dentist, the kids were napping in front of the TV. She was so pleased that Larry and I both got paid. In fact, Mrs. Jenkins gave me a glowing reference for my newspaper job.

I heard Mom come upstairs from the laundry

room and I knew this conversation was costing a heap of change. It made me long for the days when we could talk everyday for free. "Hey, Lar, I gotta go. Thanks for listening. We'll speak again soon, okay?"

"Yeah, sure. I'm glad you called. Just remember what I said. And keep me posted."

I put the receiver back on the wall and walked up to my room. Talking to Larry helped me a lot. But I still had to deal with Abner. You're probably thinking that I should have just told my parents or something. But I really hated letting them know how much I've been neglecting my school work. And telling any grown-up that someone is magically doing my assignments for me, most likely some madman, would probably land me in a psychiatrist's office. No, I had to handle this thing alone.

Mom's voice rang out. "Michael, Cara's here to see you."

I heard a groan. It came from me. "I'll be right down." Now what does she want?

Cara, it turned out, was doing a paper on the supernatural. The kid actually wanted me to take her to the house that she'd heard was haunted. She'd even written down the address.

"Let's see, where'd I put that slip of paper? Oh, here it is, right in my pocket. '200 Main Street.' Would you be able to take me there this weekend?"

She was looking at me like I was her big brother or something. I kind of always wondered what it would be like, but Cara was probably the last person I'd want to be related to. I was about to tell her that Centerville doesn't have a haunted house, that 200 Main had been checked for ghosts years ago, and that it's presently occupied. Then I had an idea. Cara could be the witness I needed. She could see some of the stunts Abner pulled and back up whatever I said about him. Maybe get him run out of town. (Whoever thinks that TV shows aren't educational is wrong.)

"Okay," I said. "How about on Sunday, around 11 o'clock?"

Cara's face lit up. "You mean it? Oh, thanks a lot!"

She ran out of the house—before I could change my mind, I guess. As I walked back to my room, I wondered if I was doing the right thing. What if Abner really went bonkers? If anything happened to Cara, it would actually be my fault. On the other hand, she asked me to take her there. Sometimes you just have to take risks in life.

Another thought occurred to me. If I knew Cara, by Sunday she'll be expert on the supernatural. Information on the subject could prove interesting, because Abner Hilks couldn't possibly be an ordinary human being. Regular people don't look like him, talk like him, or act like him. He was in a category completely unknown to me, but the more I knew, the better I could understand him. As a rule, I'm not big on snooping, but it seemed only fair; after all, the guy knew so much about me.

I decided to take Larry's advice, at least part of it. I still wanted to deliver newspapers, only not to Abner. Solution: Ask my boss, Mrs. Smith, to give 200 Main to someone else. Clever, right?

But Mrs. Smith had no record of an Abner Hilks in her computer files. In fact, she couldn't find any subscriber listed at that address.

"Isn't 200 that deserted old place, the last one on the block?"

"Yep, that's it, all right. Must be some sort of error. Sorry." I hung up the phone before she could ask me anything else. Somehow, though, I wasn't all that surprised.

Fright Time

It felt great to go on my rounds the next morning and not have to worry about seeing Abner. But school was a different story.

In math, the 10 examples I had handed in were returned. My paper was error-free. By now, this wasn't a great shock. Then Ms. Reynolds wrote a problem on the chalkboard and asked me to come up, solve it, and explain the procedure I was using. I couldn't tell if she suddenly considered me a model student who could now coach the class, or if she was suspicious about whether it was really my work she had seen.

I got up from my chair and walked slowly to the board. I wished I were somewhere else. But I picked up the chalk, cleared my throat, and decided to go with an old yet reliable ploy: the coughing fit.

"Would you like to get some water, Michael?"

I didn't dare look at Ms. Reynolds and couldn't tell from her voice if my act was convincing. In any case, I nodded and dashed from the room while someone else was chosen to replace me.

After that life-threatening tension, the cool, quiet hallway was a relief. I figured that as long as I was out there I might as well get a drink. I walked toward the nearest fountain, wishing as

I always did that it was filled with cold orange juice. As I bent over and turned the knob, I heard the unmistakable voice of Abner Hilks.

"Looks like you could use a little help in there."

I turned around fast.

"What are you doing here?"

"She'll call on you again, you know. Ms. Reynolds knows you were stalling. And all three of us are aware that you can't do the work."

"Get away from me." I tried to sound threatening, but failed miserably.

"I should think you'd want me to stay and help. It's either that or get embarrassed in front of your classmates. Not to mention letting your teacher think that you let others do your work for you."

"But I didn't know—" I heard footsteps and stopped talking. Ms. Reynolds stood in the classroom doorway.

"Everything okay, Michael?"

I could have asked her for a pass to see the school nurse, only I was too upset to pull off any more trickery. Instead I told her I was fine, and glumly went back to the classroom.

But Abner wasn't finished with me yet.

4

Okay, I'll admit it. Abner saved me. Through some kind of weird osmosis, I was able to solve a math problem for the class. And Ms. Reynolds seemed satisfied with my explanation of the procedure. Apparently, it also impressed Todd Harris, the math club president. We never had much to do with one another before, but after class, he invited me to attend the club's next meeting. Yet most important was that I finally knew beyond all doubt that it was Abner who was doing my assignments. The magic part I still didn't understand. And I still didn't know why he was doing it.

Ms. Franklin, my English teacher, was thrilled with the essay that had found its way into her basket the day before. She even asked me to read it aloud to the class—a huge compliment. I couldn't refuse or plead shyness. There's never been much evidence of that on my part. Besides, I was curious to read Abner's work.

Even I could tell that the content and writing style of the composition were really good. But what was truly amazing was that it still sounded like me, as though I'd really written it. Some of the kids actually clapped when I was through.

In science, Ken Thompson, this really bright guy, heard about my project (minutes after I did). I was flattered when he asked if he could be my partner, seeing that our topics both dealt with the human heart.

Then reality set in. I wasn't in Ken's league. I couldn't contribute anything of value, on his level. And despite Ken's smarts, he'd never understand that some bizarre phantom wrote a clear, concise outline for me. Letting myself down was bad enough but I couldn't ruin Ken's chances for a science fair prize. His disappointment would upset me, and I don't think he'd like it much either.

When I arrived home after taking the long way, I realized that things had gotten out of hand when Mom greeted me at the door with a huge smile, her eyes brimming as if she were ready to cry. I thought she'd found a million dollars or something. But apparently she'd received phone calls from Ms. Franklin and Mr. Benton about all my new improvements. Mom was so thrilled that she called Dad, who decided that going out for dinner would be a nice way to celebrate. Yes, things were getting out of hand.

When we returned from the restaurant that night, I was going into my room when I noticed something or someone huddled in the corner near my closet. With my hand shaking, I turned on the light.

What had frightened me was a pile of gym clothes that I'd forgotten to put in the hamper. I threw them in quickly, wondering how I was going to get rid of the creepy feeling I'd had since I first saw Abner Hilks. It was like he was there even when he wasn't.

I had to shake it—and him—somehow.

Friday was special, because nothing special happened. No odd creatures bothering me, no classroom surprises. Unfortunately, I couldn't quite enjoy my pleasantly uneventful day because I'd almost been waiting for something weird to pop up. Drifting off to sleep that night, I hoped this meant that Abner Hilks had left town.

I woke up on Saturday feeling good. I didn't have to deliver newspapers that weekend because some kid wanted a double route for extra money, and I had volunteered to let him have mine.

My parents were going to a party that night,

so I got driven to a video rental place to choose whatever I liked—within reason, of course. Mom hates leaving me home by myself, but I'm always pointing out that if I'm old enough to earn a living, I'm old enough to spend a night alone. That reassures her—somewhat.

I began my evening by preparing the usual feast of popcorn, pretzels, and potato chips. I pulled a can of soda from the fridge, poured it in a mug, and considered my two video selections. I really needed a comedy (you can understand why), so I went with that first.

As I was setting up the VCR in the den, I couldn't help noticing how much the house was creaking—the stairs, the ceiling, even the walls. Dad says—I once asked him—that it's just the house "settling." But this house is hardly new. You'd think it would have settled by now.

I cranked up the volume and tried to relax. I used to invite Larry over on nights like this. I remembered my appointment with Cara for Sunday. Oh, boy. Just what I didn't need. I decided to make it real fast. Abner might have left town anyway, so there was nothing for Cara to see. A quick tour around the outside of the house should do it.

Oh, great. I'd lost track of the story. I stopped

the VCR to rewind the tape a little. Then I heard those sounds again, the groaning of floorboards overhead. As if there was someone else in the house with me.

I looked at my watch. Eight o'clock. Mom and Dad wouldn't be home for several hours. Enough of this, I told myself. I found the spot where I'd lost my concentration and watched the movie.

It sure was a windy night, though. The howling was intense, and you could hear tree branches crashing into one another. At least that's what it sounded like. Then I heard something behind me, hitting the window pane. I jumped, turned around, and raised the blinds. But I couldn't see a thing, even when I pressed my face so close against the glass it fogged up.

Suddenly the vapor from my breath took the shape of a face. And suddenly, looking right at me from the other side of the window, was Abner Hilks.

5

I fumbled with the blinds, trying desperately to lower them. That done, I turned off the TV.

Madman on Main Street

NO time for comedy now. I pushed a chair against the back door. Should I call the police? That would be useless. Abner wouldn't hang around once they arrived. What about running out the front door and screaming in the street for help? Not a bad idea, except after a display of hysteria like that, Mom would insist on hiring a baby-sitter until I was 20. I definitely had to handle this myself.

The element of surprise. It works in the movies. And that's all I had going for me. But I needed a weapon, just in case. I glanced around the room. My heart was pounding so hard I couldn't think.

What was that noise? I could swear it was shuffling footsteps from the floor above. Abner? No. Why would he be upstairs? He was outside. Someone else was in the house, I was sure of it.

I still didn't have anything to defend myself with. Don't laugh, but I grabbed the first thing I saw—the remote control unit. I didn't want to hurt anyone, just zap them hard enough to buy myself some time.

The footsteps were on the stairs now, moving slowly toward the den. I needed a hiding place. My father's lounge chair seemed as good a place as any. It sat in a corner of the room and was big enough to hide me when I crouched behind it. It wasn't a fortress, but at least I could see an intruder before he could see me. I knelt on the floor and waited.

The telephone startled me. The ringing seemed endless. Finally, it stopped, only to begin again a minute later. Whoever was calling was very determined. Was it Cara asking about tomorrow's trip? At this point, I didn't know if I'd have a tomorrow. A remote control can do just so much when you're up against who knows what. Was Larry calling to see how I was? Not too great, buddy, but thanks for thinking of me. It could also be Mom, but the party she and Dad were going to was an hour's drive away, so they were probably still traveling.

The telephone, and the house, got quiet. All I could hear now was a pounding rain to accompany the loud wind. I hoped the bad weather would make Abner return to his own haunted house and leave me alone.

My legs were starting to cramp, but I didn't dare move. Then the lights went out. I didn't know if it was some sort of power failure or someone's idea of a not very funny joke. I tried the remote control to see if the TV set worked. Nothing.

I was near hysterics. This was the worst night of my life, and I couldn't understand why it was happening to me.

There was a knock at the front door. Then two more. I stood up, my legs shaking. Were those friendly knocks? I couldn't decide, until the pounding began. Definitely the sign of an enemy. Then a man's voice was calling my name. It wasn't Dad. But, it also wasn't Abner.

"Michael, are you in there? It's Mr. Mills."

Cara's father. What a relief! But I didn't want to shout back. A prowler could still be lurking, and under those circumstances, you can't be too careful.

I groped for the stairway while Mr. Mills continued to yell and pound. I could see where Cara got her loud voice. I finally reached the front door and opened it.

"Michael, thank goodness. I was getting worried. Were you sleeping?"

"No, I, uh . . ." What could I say? That a strange old guy with magical powers has been bothering me? And I've been hiding from him, or perhaps some other crazed person who enjoys frightening kids on a Saturday night?

FRIGHT TIME

"Look, your Mom called us. She and your Dad have car trouble and need to stay over. You're to spend the night with us. That, and I quote, is an order. I was told you'd put up a fuss, but being here alone is absolutely out of the question."

"Okay."

Mr. Mills looked surprised. "Take my flashlight. I'll wait here while you go get your things." He stepped into the foyer. "Your parents tried phoning you but they said there was no answer. Didn't you hear it ringing?"

I mumbled something about not being able to come to the phone. Usually when people say that, it means they were in the bathroom. I felt embarrassed, but at least it stopped further questioning. I grabbed my pajamas, clothes for Sunday, and my toothbrush. Then I dumped everything in a plastic bag that was lying around and flew down the stairs.

"I'm ready."

"You'll need a jacket."

"Oh, right." I opened the coat closet and took the first thing I saw. No good. It was my mother's. My second try was more successful. "Let's go."

Cara and Mrs. Mills were in the kitchen waiting for us. We snacked on cookies and milk while discussing the awful storm. Mr. Mills telephoned Mom and Dad and assured them that I was safe. Then he passed the phone to me. They said that they expected to be home by Sunday afternoon.

While Mrs. Mills set up the living room's sofa bed for me, Cara and I stayed in the kitchen. I used the opportunity to ask the kid some questions.

"So how're you doing with that report? The one on the supernatural?"

"Good. I've got lots of information, mostly from library books." She lowered her voice. "You're still going with me tomorrow, aren't you? To that Main Street house?"

"Sure, if the weather clears up." I was practically whispering.

"Listen, I've got this friend. He's a real nice guy but he's got a real weird problem. No one would believe it. In fact, I'd doubt the story myself, if my perfectly sane friend hadn't told it to me."

Cara's eyes widened. "Told you what?"

"Well, he met this old man, a real oddball, who . . . seems to have magical powers. I know it sounds crazy, but the guy pops up out of nowhere, vanishes just as quickly, and retrieves things without blinking an eye."

"Wow."

So far, so good, I thought. The kid wasn't running to her parents yet, screaming that I was a lunatic. "Now, here comes the really strange part. This man has been handing in homework that my friend has forgotten to do, and acing tests that he never studied for. It may sound like a good deal, but things are getting out of control."

"What do you mean?" she asked.

I must say, Cara was taking this well. "Well, for one thing, my friend doesn't like fooling his parents, his teachers, and his classmates. And this kook has already hinted that he wants something in return, only he's taking his time, waiting for the right moment to spring it on him." I took a deep breath. "What I want to know is, have you read about this sort of thing in your research books?"

"Yep. Sounds like you've got yourself some kind of madman. They're capable of anything."

"How could you tell?" I asked her.

"The disappearing, the hocus-pocus—"

"No, I meant, that it was me, not some friend."

"It wasn't hard. I saw your wonderful test paper, remember? And from the way your mother acted, I got the feeling that good grades don't often happen. No offense."

"None taken."

Mrs. Mills came into the kitchen to announce that the sofa bed was ready and that we should get some sleep. Which was fine with me. I was beat.

I was half-asleep when I heard the eerie voice of Abner Hilks.

I sat up and stared. There he was.

"Good evening, Michael. How nice to see you again."

"Well, it isn't nice to see you. Stop bothering me. I'm trying to sleep."

Abner laughed his freakish laugh. "Sleep? You're not here to sleep."

"What are you talking about?" Then I looked around. I was sitting on a throne-like chair, not a sofa bed in my neighbors' living room. And I was in a dark and dingy castle—more like a dungeon, really. Instead of wearing my familiar pajamas, I was dressed in a brown robe with a hood. A gold rope was at my waist, and I wore gold slippers that curled up at the tips. Yikes. If the JV team saw me, I'd never live it down in a million years.

"What's going on here? Where am I?"

"You're in my chambers. I should think you'd be pleased. It's quite an honor, you know."

"Honor someone else. Is this still Centerville?" I looked around for a telephone. Calling the police while Abner's back was turned would definitely be Plan A.

"Of course not. What would one with my powers be doing in such an ordinary place?"

Good question, I thought. Cara was right; Abner was some kind of nut. Now I knew what I was dealing with, but would it help me any?

Don't show fear, I told myself. With whatever courage I had, I said, "I think you'd better tell me what you want. Fast."

"There's no hurry. You're not going anywhere. But if you must know, I need an apprentice. Someone to help me in my work, now that I'm getting on in years."

Getting on in years? Talk about an understatement. The guy must have been born three centuries ago. But that wasn't the problem.

I had to get out of there. I looked around for an escape, yet I didn't even see a window.

"Looking for a window?" Mind reading, in my opinion, is the worst invasion of privacy. That Abner could do it gave me the creeps. Then he waved his arms. "Poof. A window." He cackled hysterically. He should try toning that down, I thought. Too cornball.

I got up from the chair and peered out. No, we weren't in Centerville. We weren't even on solid ground. This dump was sitting on an endless bank of clouds.

"Go ahead. Yell, run for help, do whatever you want. No one will hear you. No one will see you." He waved his pointy fingertips at me. "Frankly, I'm a bit insulted that you'd want to leave."

"Don't take it personally. It's just that my parents will worry. And there's this kid at school, we're supposed to do a project together for the science fair. He's counting on me."

"Well, if you can find the way back to Centerville from here, you're better than I. Hah, hah, hah." Then, in a flash, he disappeared.

Despite all the obstacles, I couldn't accept defeat. There had to be a solution. But the question was, how'd I ever get into this mess? Wait, what was that?

"Psst, Michael. Over here."

"Larry!" I spun around. I didn't see anyone, but my friend's voice seemed to be coming from a wall, behind a portrait of Abner. It must have been painted by some fake because, trust me, the old guy never looked that good. "Where are you?" I asked my friend.

"Hurry! There's no time. Take down Abner's portrait. You'll find a key stuck to the back of it," he answered.

I lifted the heavy painting, nearly choking from the dirt and cobwebs that flew around. Gee, I thought, doesn't anyone dust around here? Just as Larry said, there was an old key glued to the canvas. I tugged and finally pried it loose.

"Okay. Got it," I said.

"Keep your voice down," Larry said. "Or they'll hear you. Now, see those rows of bookshelves?" I hadn't even noticed them before, but they took up an entire wall. "On the third shelf, behind the books, you'll see a lock. Slide the key in and turn it to the left," Larry directed me.

I did as he told me. To my amazement, a section of the wall slowly opened. And Larry was on the other side!

"Am I glad to see you!" I greeted him.

"Me, too. But really, we don't have a second to spare. Close the door behind you."

"Where are we doing?" I asked.

"Through this passageway. It's a tunnel that will take us back to earth."

"How do you know all this?" Larry was walking so fast I practically had to run to keep up with him. "How long have you been here? We just spoke on the phone a few days ago."

"I'll tell you everything later. Come on. Hurry."

The place was dark and damp, I was scared, and I knew Larry was too. Then suddenly a voice boomed, "And where do you think you're going?"

My heart fell. Out of nowhere, Abner appeared in front of us, nearly covered by a foggy haze. His face was frozen in anger, his crossed arms were pressed tightly to his chest. I hadn't noticed it before, but on his pinky was a huge diamond ring. The ring gave off a light so strong I had to shield my eyes from it.

"Follow me, boys."

7

"No!" I screamed over and over, still needing to cover my eyes. "No!"

"Michael, Michael, it's okay. Wake up."

I managed to raise an eyelid. I was back on the sofa bed, looking into the worried faces of Mr. and Mrs. Mills, Cara, and even little Beth. I sat up quickly, the bright sunshine warming my back. I felt dazed and confused.

"That must have been some nightmare," Cara said.

"No, a daymare!" squealed Beth, giggling at her joke.

"Are you okay, Michael?" asked Mrs. Mills. Her voiced sounded worried.

I just nodded, wishing I were home with my parents. If you're going to yell like a nut while a horrible dream plays in your brain, it's best to do so among your own family.

"Come on, let's let Michael get ready for my super colossal Sunday breakfast," said Mr. Mills. "Everyone out."

Cara was the last to leave. "The weather's perfect, Michael." Then she whispered, "Perfect for haunted-house hunting."

I groaned. Great, I thought. How can I tell this girl, who's younger than I am, that wild horses wouldn't get me anywhere near 200 Main Street?

I thought of stalling until my folks got home, then using my reunion with them as an excuse for not going. But Cara was a pretty good kid, and it wouldn't be right to treat her that way. And, after washing, putting on clean clothes, and enjoying a huge breakfast, I was in a much better frame of mind.

My bicycle was at home, so Cara and I planned to meet in front of her driveway. I walked toward our garage. We have one of those security things where you press a combination of numbers on a panel on the garage door. I could never forget our secret code: It was my birthday. I always got a charge out of how the whole thing worked. It's like magic. You just push a few buttons and within seconds this heavy steel door is raised without your lifting a finger. Well, you do lift a finger for the buttons, but you know what I mean.

Anyway, the garage door opened, same as always. I walked to my bike, ready to hit the kickstand, when suddenly the door snapped shut. It's not supposed to do that. Now the place was dark and I was not pleased.

"Off on a jaunt, are you?" That voice of his again!

I couldn't see Abner, but he was there all right. "Look, this is private property. Either go away and never come back or I'm going to call the police," I said.

"But I'm your friend, my lad. No doubt the best you've got. I hope you remember all the favors I've done for you."

"I'm not your lad or your anything else," I said, "and I never asked you for favors."

"Nor did you ask that I stop granting them. You knew it was my efforts your teachers were seeing."

"I also know that we're not friends. So what are you after, my paper route money? I've already spent most of it."

That tickled Abner. I was almost sorry I mentioned it; he needed a full minute to settle down. Then he grew serious.

"I want the secret access code to the newspaper's computer."

I thought I was hearing things. This was all

about Centerville's newspaper? "Why?"

"I'm not at liberty to say."

"You're at liberty to say, all right. You just don't want to. Anyway, it doesn't matter, because I don't know about computer access codes. I'm just a paper boy."

"You'd merely have to ask an adult employed at the office for the information I'm seeking."

"They'd want to know why I want it, same as I've asked you."

"You can make up some excuse. I've seen you do that before. In fact, you're quite good at it."

"Michael! Are you in there?" It was Cara, in the driveway it sounded like.

"Be right out," I shouted. To Abner I said, "What if I refuse?"

"Your grades will fall. Your parents will be so disappointed. Rumors may spread that someone's been doing your work for you, that you're a cheat. Children and neighbors will talk about you."

"I get the picture." I was sweating. "Open the garage door. Please."

"Think carefully about what I've said. Much depends on it. And remember this: I can be a helpful friend or a terrible enemy."

FRIGHT TIME

The door opened and the warm sunlight flooded the garage. Abner was gone. I walked outside and breathed deeply.

"What took you so long?"

"Sorry." I really didn't know what to say to her. "Cara, even though visiting that house means a lot to you, maybe it's not such a good idea."

"Why? You said—"

"I know, but you can't tell about things like this. It could be dangerous." Cara wore such a puzzled expression that I wound up telling her about my latest run-in with Abner. She reacted with more gumption than I expected.

"Michael, you have to report this to the police."

"Yeah, right. Like they'll really believe me."

"I'll go with you."

"What for? I'm the only one who's ever seen Abner. They'll probably think I'm this wiseguy trying to fool them and a little kid. No offense."

"None taken." She grinned. "Come on. Between the two of us, we might convince a patrol officer to take us through the house. That way I'll have something for my report, and maybe this Abner person will go haunt some other town."

A sensible argument, I must admit. There was just one matter to discuss. "Uh, Cara, let's not mention this business to anyone. It may cause more problems than I already have."

"Fair enough. Okay, it's off to the police station. You lead, I'll follow."

On the way over, I had a funny feeling about what we were doing. I'd never been in Centerville's police station before. I've never even wanted to be. What if I walked in there, just to say hi or something, and some kid with a mean-looking parent says, "That's him. That's the boy who stole my bicycle!" It could happen, you know. You hear about mistaken identity all the time. But I had to risk it.

Cara and I rode up to the station house. We didn't bother to lock up our bikes. Who'd be stupid enough to swipe them? Anyway, we went inside and headed for the main desk, where an Officer Taylor was on the phone. Then he hung up and asked if he could help us.

I gulped and said, "We'd like to report—" I was suddenly tongue-tied, watching Officer Taylor's eyes bore right into mine.

FRIGHT TIME

Cara took over. "We'd like to report a—" She caught herself. "A weird person."

Officer Taylor rubbed his forehead. "Someone's bothering you kids?"

I jumped back in again. "Just me, I guess."

"What's this person's name?"

"Abner Hilks."

"Don't think I know him."

"He's new in town," Cara said.

"What sort of things is he doing?"

Cara again. "Michael's homework, tests..."

I poked her. Officer Taylor's eyes were narrowing. Not a good sign. "He's been sort of threatening me."

"Have you told your folks? You'll need one of them or a guardian to file a complaint, you know."

"His parents are out of town," Cara said.

"I see. Well, I can't do much right now. But I will ask around about this Mr. Hilks. Do you know his address?"

Here it comes. The disbelief, the funny look, the lecture about joking to a police officer. "He lives at 200 Main Street."

"Someone moved into that dump? Hmmm. Okay, we'll keep our eyes open. Meanwhile, you kids take care, you hear?"

We promised to do so and left. I felt relieved, because I'd done something actual and reported Abner to a police officer, even if it was unofficially. I was just about to hop on my bike when I realized something. Something awful.

"Hey, Cara, what if Abner knows we've been here? I mean, he's found out about everything else. What if he gets angry and decides to do something?"

Cara looked at me as though I were dense. "Do you think he cares about the police?"

"Maybe not in the same way normal humans do. But he is touchy. He could be teed off that we tried to get the law after him."

"Maybe you're right." She stopped to think. "I have an idea. It's risky, but it could work. It's worth a try, anyway."

"Let's hear it."

"Tell Abner how he can find the computer access code."

"Why would I do that?"

"To get him out of his house. If we can get in, there could be clues all over the place. We can learn a lot, more than he'll ever tell you, I'll bet."

"What do I say to him?"

"It's simple. Make up a code, some letters, throw in a number or two. When he can't gain access to the paper's system and complains later, say you misunderstood, you didn't jot the code down correctly, something like that."

"But he'll just keep pestering me."

"You can say that if you annoy the busy newspaper staff again, you could lose your job, which you need very badly."

Cara's plan sounded good—if it worked. But failure could be disastrous.

9

The plan was in motion. Cara and I hid behind some bushes, watching Abner leave the Main Street house. I couldn't believe how easy it'd been—at least so far. All I did was slip a note under Abner's front door, ring the bell, and hop on my bike before he saw me. Among my primary goals on this mission was to avoid any face-to-face encounter with him if I could.

We waited until Abner was out of sight. Then we raced to the back of the house. I headed for the door that I remembered being there and turned the knob. It was open!

Cara whispered, "I wonder what the jail time is for trespassing?"

"I'm sure Abner's not supposed to be here, either, so don't worry." Nevertheless, we walked in quietly. No sense disturbing any of Abner's friends or relatives, if any.

The place looked worse from the inside, worse than the last time I was there. Huge cobwebs hung from the ceiling. Dust on the few pieces of furniture was about an inch thick. The air had a stale, choky quality, as though there hadn't been a window opened in years. Luckily, we'd brought flashlights, because in spite of the still sunny day, the house on 200 Main Street was dark. Even at midnight, the place wouldn't look much different.

We were at the front of the house now. If there were clues of any kind, they were well hidden. A long staircase led to the top floor. I looked at Cara. Should we climb it? I still felt responsible for her. I mean, Mr. and Mrs. Mills have been really nice to me. I'd never forgive myself . . . I shuddered at the thought.

Then Cara nudged me. "Over there. It looks like a study."

She was right. And it was the only area that

showed any signs of recent activity. Piles of books were everywhere. Large candlesticks stood on shelves and bookcases and a huge desk. Apparently this is where Abner spent much of his time.

I moved to the desk to see what Abner was reading. Interesting. A book on the human heart, obviously used to help me with my science project. There was a volume on the historical period we were studying in Mr. Benton's class. I guess there's no free lunch for wizards either. I mean, crazy Abner was making a real effort for me.

What was I thinking? He didn't do anything to help me! He was just trying to make me feel grateful, obligated, even afraid. It was all part of this scheme of his. And I was supposed to be an accomplice.

Why did he pick me? I could answer that now. Because I wasn't doing my work, I put myself in a desperate situation. And desperate people do desperate things. Looking back, I had to admit I was the perfect candidate for Abner's job.

Cara brought me back to the present. "Look at this!" She showed me an opened notebook. On the front page, in Abner's old-fashioned handwriting, were these words: *Plan to Rule Center-*

ville. I was as shocked as Cara. I was expecting something, but not this!

I flipped through the pages, getting an idea of Abner's crazed plan: to win over Centerville's citizens through our town's only newspaper. Secretly using the computer, he planned to revise and rewrite articles that would introduce Abner Hilks to the people here. Then, his messages would become stronger. That everyone would be better off with him running the town. That there'd be no unemployment, no crime, nothing but a carefree existence under his rule. His rule! What baloney.

"It's nice to see you reading, Michael. Pity you chose something that is clearly private and personal."

Why was I surprised? Abner had this habit of showing up unexpectedly. My hands shook, regardless, to the point where I dropped the notebook.

Cara tried to hide her fear, but it was there all right. "Personal? You call a plan to take over Centerville and control its people, personal? Well, here's a news flash—anything that affects an entire community isn't personal."

"Yeah," I chimed in. Great, Michael, I thought. Well, I had to say something.

"This town is better than others I've visited. But it could be so much more. Just like Michael, Centerville has so much potential. The potential to become a utopia, a perfect place to grow up in, to run a business, to enjoy leisure time. A town to spend a lifetime of peace and harmony."

Abner was persuasive, I'll give him that. He almost had me convinced. Perfect lives for one and all? Sounded good to me. But at what price?

Cara read my mind. "What would people have to do for all this peace and harmony?"

"Obey my rules. A fair exchange, in my opinion."

Then he turned to me. "I'm very upset with you, Michael. I chose you to help me. Instead you're trying to destroy my plan. Now I'll have to destroy you. And your friend."

10

Abner waved his hand and produced a lit candle. My worst fears were coming true. I looked at Cara. Tears were filling her eyes.

"Let her go, Abner. She can't hurt you. I don't care about myself. Just let her go."

"A noble gesture. I'm impressed." He looked at Cara. "Pity, she is quite young. But unfortunately, she knows too much." His face hardened. "This way. Now."

He led us down a narrow flight of stairs. I took Cara's hand. It was the least I could do. Poor kid. What a way to go.

Suddenly, I got real mad. I was even angrier than I was scared. Why should we let a creep like Abner decide our fate? Just who did he think he was?

Giving in to my anger, I hit him on the head with my flashlight as hard as I could. But he had no reaction, probably because he didn't feel anything. Unbelievable. I guess wizards are really built differently than humans. Maybe it was just as well, because if he had felt or seen what I'd done, there's no telling what he might have done to us.

He took us down to a cellar. Good thing that it was so dark, because I could just about imagine the horrors that were down there. Cara refused to sit on the floor, and insisted that Abner bring us chairs. No problem. He snapped his fingers and, bingo, two chairs.

"What are you going to do with us?" I asked him. As a rule, I'm not big on surprises. Whenever possible, it's good to know what a crazy wizard has in store for you.

"An excellent question, but one I can't answer yet. You see, I haven't quite decided. I was thinking that you and your friend would make excellent hostages. I'm certain the town would forfeit governmental power in exchange for two children."

This made me feel better. Because if he wanted to, I knew Abner could just wave his hand and make us disappear. The way I figured, the more time we had, the greater our chances of getting out—alive.

"If you need anything else, just yell. Not that it will do you a bit of good." Abner chuckled fiendishly as he marched up the stairs.

Cara sounded weepy. "This is my fault, Michael. I'm sorry."

"No, it's Abner's fault, for being a power-hungry madman, or mad wizard, or whatever. Hey, cheer up. Our parents will be looking for us soon. They'll probably call the police station. Maybe they'll even speak to that Officer Taylor. Maybe he already discussed what we said with his pals on the force. Maybe they're doing some investigating right now."

"That's a lot of maybe's."

"Well, look on the bright side. At least you've got some interesting material for your report."

"Right now that's the furthest thing from my mind."

"It shouldn't be."

"Are you serious? We're in deep trouble, Michael."

"Think back for a minute. You did a lot of reading and stuff for your project, correct?"

"Sure."

"Did you come across anything about killing a mad wizard?"

Cara thought for a moment. "No. But remember the movie where the witch shriveled down to nothing after a bucket of water was thrown on her? That could work."

I remembered last night, when Abner stood outside my window. Once the storm began, he was gone. Then again, even I know enough to come in out of the rain. "It sounds a little too easy, but it's worth a try."

"Not that easy. I doubt this place has running

water," Cara said.

I had to see just how bad a mess we were in. Turning on my flashlight, I stood and walked quietly around the room. It was some dump. If anything could give you nightmares, it was this dungeon. In fact, to make sure you don't suffer on my account, I'll eliminate the gruesome details.

I spun around.

I thought I heard someone call my name. I stopped and listened. Yes! Unbelievable! He was here—my buddy, my best friend. He'd come and found us!

"Down here, Larry. In the basement!" I was shouting, but so what. Our lives were at stake. And, come to think of it, so was our whole town.

Larry's voice was closer now. "Okay, I know where you are. Hang tight. I'll get you out."

This was so bizarre—Larry showing up, just like in my dream.

Cara had met Larry when she and her parents bought the house he used to live in. She was really relieved that help was on the way.

Good old Larry. If anyone could get us out of this, it was my pal.

Cara and I waited for what seemed like a long time. Then the cellar door opened. My heart nearly stopped when I saw Abner pushing Larry down the stairs.

11

From the way Larry acted, you'd think that getting kidnapped by a wizard was an everyday thing for him. But he held an orange drink and it was shaking. Badly enough to be foaming at the top.

"You children have some company," Abner said. He was really enjoying this. "I found this young pup snooping around my yard."

I wanted to throw something. Pup? *His* yard? Give me a break.

"Make yourself at home, lad. I'd love to stay and chat, but I've lots to do." Abner scurried upstairs. I was never so glad to see him go.

Larry grinned at Cara and me. It was terrific seeing him, despite the circumstances. "You described him perfectly, Michael. What a loon." We laughed as Larry imitated Abner. Then my buddy and I shook hands.

"I can't believe this. What are you doing here?" I asked.

FRIGHT TIME

"I could ask you the same thing. My parents and I are in town visiting my grandmother. I heard about the trip just this morning and phoned you, but no one answered. Anyway, I ran to your house as soon as I could, just as your parents were pulling into the driveway. They said you were at Cara's, but when I went there, her folks told me that you both went bike riding. I think they're a little worried."

With good reason, I thought. "Well, I guess the first order of business is to find a way out of here. Any ideas?"

"We outnumber Abner," Larry said. "That ought to count for something."

"His powers count for more," Cara replied. "He *is* a wizard, don't forget, besides being a maniac."

"Let's break that amazingly filthy window," I said. "This flashlight could do the job."

"Too noisy," Larry said. "Why don't we look around for a trap door or something? Maybe there's one that Abner doesn't know about."

We agreed to search, which at least kept us busy. While looking for a safe escape route, I started to feel ashamed. This whole mess began with me. Now, thanks to my blabbering, I'd endangered my best friend and my next-door neighbor. I shouldn't have told them anything. I should have kept it all to myself, handled Abner on my own. Well, I thought, what's done is done. But it was my responsibility to save Cara and Larry, no matter what.

I wondered if Abner locked the cellar door after he brought Larry down. He did seem kind of distracted. Holding my breath, trying to be quiet, I inched my way to the top of the staircase. I turned the doorknob. It was locked. But the hinges didn't seem very sturdy. Maybe we could unfasten them.

I didn't dare risk going back and hitting one of the squeaky steps. Instead I whispered to Cara and Larry, asking them to look for something that could unbolt the door. Cara had a barrette, only it wasn't strong enough to hold up to my frantic twists and turns.

Larry noticed drops of water coming from an exposed pipe. "Let's save them," he said. "The water probably isn't safe for drinking, but it could be useful."

I found a bucket and handed it to Cara. "We could test your water theory."

"Okay." She placed the bucket under the pipe, until the sound of droplets hitting tin grew too noisy. Then Cara took a rag that was lying on the floor and lined the pail's bottom to muffle the noise. It would take longer now, what with the rag absorbing the moisture. But Cara's sad expression and manner bothered me more than anything. I could tell that she was wondering the same thing I was: Would we ever get out of here? Out of sheer frustration, I kicked a wooden support beam. The thing was so old that it shook the entire building. It very well may have, because it sent Abner scurrying to the cellar. He was furious.

"There's far too much activity going on down here. Is this the thanks I get for treating you children fairly?"

"Fair—?" I sputtered. I could barely speak, I was so angry.

"It's too late for apologies now," Abner interrupted. "I've learned my lesson." He winked at me.

Yeah, Abner, I get it. Very funny. Then he waved his hand and produced a long rope. He pointed to Cara and crooked his forefinger for her to approach him. She hid behind me.

"I told you, Abner. Leave her alone."

"Oh, really, Michael. Haven't you realized

that if I were going to hurt anyone I'd have done it long ago? Tying you all to this pole is for your own good. It'll keep you out of trouble." He stepped forward and held out his hand to Cara. "Now, my dear, if you would be so kind."

Larry had moved closer to me also. Still clutching his orange drink in one hand, he made a move for the flashlight I was holding. I knew what he wanted—to bop Abner over the head with the instrument—but I couldn't very well tell him it was useless.

Instead I tried to discourage him by clenching the flashlight even tighter. He didn't understand, which resulted in a struggle. Before we realized it, Larry's orange drink slipped from his grasp and spilled all over Abner.

We were afraid to budge. I expected some reaction, but not the screech that filled the room. It was Abner, howling and writhing in pain! "Help me," he managed to utter. "My skin is on fi-i-r-e."

There were no flames, but I heard a crackling sound and sniffed what had to be the odor of burning flesh. Then, before our eyes, Abner slowly started to shrivel away. "The acid!" he howled. "The acid is burning my flesh!"

It was a horrifying sight. The three of us were

speechless. We couldn't move. Finally Cara picked up the now empty drink container and examined the label. "It was the acid," she said. "There's ascorbic acid in the orange drink. Abner's body isn't—wasn't— like a human's. The spilled liquid burned it."

Larry sighed. "Let's get out of here before something else happens. Where's that window?"

After moving a pile of stuff that was lying beneath the dirty window, we dragged over the chairs that Abner had conjured up for us. But they kept wobbling, as if they were on bumpy terrain. I shined the flashlight on the floor and saw that the chairs had been resting on an old tombstone. I knelt down beside it and saw the inscription etched in granite: HERE LIES THE ETERNAL SPIRIT OF ABNER HILKS. No dates, no loving words.

I had to wonder: Was Abner a wizard who actually lived here? Was he the relative of some other Abner Hilks? Or did he take on the name of a dead person for reasons only he could have answered?

Cara and I held the chairs steady while Larry discovered the window's latch. To our surprise, it wasn't locked, just stiff from disuse. After some hard work, the thing actually opened.

Larry scrambled out; Cara was next. Just before it was my turn, I wandered over to where Abner last stood, searching for his remains. But there was nothing. Nothing at all.

Not even a stain to show where he had been.

12

Maybe supernatural beings like Abner never really die. Perhaps they have some kind of life of their own, going on in one way or another.

Despite everything that happened, I can't say that I'm sorry I met Abner Hilks. He made me aware of another dimension, a part of the world I now believe exists.

Would he have really harmed my friends and me? I don't know for sure. I do think that he wanted to govern—in his way, by his rules—a small town like Centerville. Can't blame the guy, I guess. It's a nice place, with nice people. Maybe his intentions were honorable, and he just went after his goal, something he wanted very badly, the wrong way. Humans do, too, when you stop to think about it.

It's also possible that Abner looked for respect

and attention, that he wanted a whole town's worth of people to admire him. There are plenty of humans like that, too. Looking back, I can understand why he was so upset with me. I ruined his dream, a dream that sheer magic couldn't fulfill.

One thing I especially remember about Abner was his always quoting "Knowledge is power." For him, I suppose power was the key word. But I think something in him wanted me to know the saying for its other meaning: That learning is good, that education is important.

As a kind of tribute to my former opponent, I've been working hard, doing my assignments on time and as best I can. I, Michael Dane, am still not the world's greatest student. But thanks to old Abner, I'm a much better one.

It's Almost Dark

by Jane Ehlers

1

Spencer and I have been hanging out together for as long as I can remember. Nobody knows the Kadison family better than I do—I stay at Spencer's house all the time. "You're really weird, Spence," I always tell him. He is, too.

"I know," he always says, and he always pushes his glasses higher up on his nose—especially when he gets embarrassed—that is, when he's not forgetting them somewhere, which is pretty much all the time.

"You're definitely weird."

"Runs in the family," he says.

They *are* weird. All of them. When we were in fifth grade, somebody told Spence his mom looks like the kind of mom in spooky movies or TV shows. When Spence told his mom that, she laughed and said it was a compliment. She thought it was cool.

Spencer's mom has really long dark hair and she wears black a lot—maybe that's why people think she looks like she's from a movie. She's an artist, and she tells fortunes from tarot cards at their house. She gives "readings" for people, in the sunroom, as she calls it, at an old wicker table covered with a faded shawl with a long fringe.

Mrs. K. has a lot of candles. She keeps them everywhere. There are always a few candles burning—flickering in colored glass holders.

Spencer's dad writes kids' books, and draws the pictures for them himself. He invents really weird games, too, and he works at his computer a lot.

One time, he was writing this story about goblins, and the pictures he drew were really bizarre, scarier than his usual stories. That was when I really knew the Kadisons are sort of—

well, *different*. And that was when I saw some stuff I wish I'd never seen.

"What *is* that smell, Dan?" Spencer's mom called. Dan is Spencer's dad. I'd slept over. Mrs. K. was stepping lightly around their enormous cat, Beardsley, and picking up colored plastic shapes, alphabet letters, and a lot of fuzzy little creatures and dolls from the living room floor—Shannon's stuff.

Shannon is Spencer's little sister. I guess she was about three or four when Mr. K. was working on the goblin book. "Ever since you started working on that story," Mrs. K. called to Mr. K., "there's been a weird odor around your drawing board. It comes and goes. Did you spill something on the rug in there?" She came into the studio fanning her hand in front of her face as if waving away some big-time toxic waste.

Dan Kadison always stays up late at night working on his pictures, scanning stuff into the computer through the picture scanner, printing out his pictures, faxing stuff to people. He'd been drawing these gnome-like, wrinkled little squinty guys with pointed ears and dried leaves and damp-looking moss that clung to their bodies like messy little caveman suits. These creepy creatures gave off steam when they moved. They had matted, awful-looking hair, and scowly faces, too.

Spence and I always sneak a peek at Mr. K.'s pictures when he leaves the studio. We peered at the deformed little people. "Yuck," I said. We studied the drawings for a while. Mr. K. had been putting in the color.

Spencer poked me with his elbow. "There's that smell again," he said. I remember thinking that it might have been the paints.

"Yikes!" I jumped a mile. Mr. K. grabbed my shoulders, yanking my shirt. Spence and I were laughing—Mr. K. was hunching himself over and shuffling around the studio, dragging one leg, coming at us, reaching out with one hand curled into a claw. I was startled, though. It felt like a baseball was suddenly jammed into my throat. "They follow you around, you know," he went on, scowling and gritting his teeth, still coming at us while he made these faces.

"Da-a-ad," Spencer whined, pushing his glasses up with one finger. "Stop!"

"They hide behind trees and wait for you to come home," he said, glancing out the window.

It's Almost Dark

The Kadisons have a gigantic backyard, lots of space, with woods in back. Mr. K. peered out the window. I began to wonder if he really thought there were goblins out there. "They slip in really fast—right behind you—when you open the door," he said, always the storyteller. "That's how they get in."

I jumped again. Mr. K.'s laser printer had begun to whir suddenly, and paper began slowly sliding out of it. It kind of reminded me of toothpaste oozing from the tube. We peeked at the pages while Mr. K.'s back was turned. They were copies of his murky, mysterious goblin pictures.

Spence and I looked at each other. He was pushing at his glasses again. It was funny, the story about the goblins; but then, in a way, it wasn't. And I thought I smelled a moldy kind of smell as Mr. K. lurched around the studio. He hadn't even noticed that the printer was running. He was in his own picture-book world. "Once they're in the house," he said, "well . . ." He paused, then went on, "it's the beds you've got to watch. They get under the beds. Into the closet, too. And behind stuff, like back here." He passed his arm behind a file cabinet, up to his shoulder, and pretended to grope around. Then he went into a spasm.

I jumped again. We thought something had bitten him. "Just kidding," he said, chuckling. I felt like an idiot. "I'm telling you, guys," Mr. K. said, "this new scanner I put in is unbelievable! It really puts out lifelike images. My goblins are printing out totally scary! So what do you think, Ben?" Mr. K. moved toward the drawing board and loomed over my shoulder, looking at his latest goblin picture.

"Awesome," I said, backing away from him a little. That baseball had swelled into my throat again. Then my mom called to remind me to come home and finish my homework before dinner. It was Sunday, and we were supposed to have company coming over. I mean, I like Spence and all, but I was beginning to feel kind of creepy. Suddenly, Sunday company and homework seemed like sort of a relief.

I wheeled my bike out of the Kadisons' garage, and I rode home really fast.

"Wait, Ben, my glasses..." Spencer darted back out onto the gym floor. Gym class was over, and he'd left his glasses on the mat, as always. It's a wonder they never get stepped on.

It's Almost Dark

I was already dressed. Spencer was shrugging into his red flannel shirt. Something was sticking out of the pocket. "What's this?" I asked him, pulling it out. I turned it over in my hand. It was a leaf, crinkly and dry, with some sort of stringy moss stuck to it.

"I don't know," he said. "C'mon. I'm starved."

"Wait up," I called after him, tossing the leaf into the trash as I ran out of the locker room. He must have been rolling around in the leaves out back, I thought.

It was getting dark earlier now. Halloween was over. Heading home from school, Spence and I always go through the playground. Most of the trees were already bare. Every year it seems that every leaf on earth blows into our town. We shuffle through them on the way home, knee-deep sometimes. Probably how that leaf got into his pocket, I thought that day, watching Spencer plowing through a big pile of them. I couldn't figure out what that mossy stuff was that was stuck on the leaf, though.

"Mom?" Spencer dropped his knapsack down loudly on the mudroom floor. I always go there first after school. I hung my jacket on a peg.

FRIGHT TIME

Beardsley tiptoed over to me, winding himself around my ankles a few times. He's definitely the fattest cat in the hemisphere. "He thinks he's a dog," Spencer always says. "Mom?" he called again.

We peered into the sunroom. Mrs. K. was doing a card reading at the table across from a lady sitting with her. Their soft voices sounded like far-off singing, but I couldn't hear the words.

"Maybe your mom can tell what I'm getting for Christmas," I said to Spence. We snorted, squeezing our lips closed to stifle our laughter.

"Yeah, right." He pulled me back into the kitchen and rummaged around in a cabinet, bringing out a bag of pretzels.

"No cookies?" I was starting to say when Mr. K. came out of the studio with Beardsley trailing behind him.

"Hands," he said. Mr. K. always says that when he wants us to wash before eating. "Hey, guys," Mr. K. said, "I want to show you something. Walk this way!" Mr. K. started doing his monster-walk again, leading us down the hall and into the studio, pretending to be Frankenstein or something.

He sat down at his computer. He was designing a new computer game, something about android warriors—part living, part robot—who come from the future. Scientists ought to study Mr. K.'s brain. It's so cool. He showed us the warriors he was working on.

The head warrior was an awesome combination of a Viking, a knight in armor, and a cop who time-travels by computer through cyberspace—you know—the information superhighway. He has everything—monster headgear with a night-vision visor, geographical-scanning grid, a sword made of some metal we haven't discovered yet, a laser device to deter bad guys. He can even launch fireballs from some kind of thing built into his forearm. He wears part armor, part animal skin. I didn't realize it then, but his name would stick with me for quite a while—Tarx.

"Well, guys, what do you think?" Mr. K. asked enthusiastically.

"He's totally outrageous, Dad," Spence said. "Hey, Dad—what's that funny smell, anyway? Do you smell that?"

Mr. K. didn't answer. He was completely caught up in his work again, and was staring into the computer screen.

"Dad? Dad..." Spencer started again. But then Beardsley let out this sudden snarling, spitting noise.

"Beardsley?" Startled, Mr. K. looked down at his feet. Beardsley was crouched there with his ears turned flat against his head. He was showing his teeth, as if maybe he was about to pounce on a mouse or something.

"Why is he growling?" Spencer asked.

For some reason, that tingle went up my back again. "Time to go," I blurted out. "Homework." The homework excuse again. It was getting dark out, anyway.

I went back out to the mudroom for my jacket. Alone for a second, I thought I heard a kind of shuffling sound. I craned my neck to look behind the washing machine. There it was again. Mice?

"Lose something?" I spun around, startled. I hadn't heard Mr. K. come in. He chuckled. "Spence will see you out."

As we went out to the driveway, I heard a hollow clunk sound coming from the dryer, as if there were something knocking around inside it. I felt a sort of sting in my nose, like smoke and that smell again. Spencer didn't seem to notice it, I guess because he was already outside.

"See you," he called after me. I walked a little faster. When I knew he couldn't see me any more, I ran. And I ran the rest of the way home.

2

It wasn't long before I was hanging out at Spencer's as usual. It wasn't too hard to convince myself I had just let myself get spooked the last time I was over there, like when Mr. K. was kidding us about the goblins, or when the printer kicked on and his weird, murky pictures started sliding out. Or when I'd heard that noise in the mudroom.

The Kadisons have a lot of cool games for their computer. One day Spence and I were into this ancient warrior game with knights in armor and stuff, when the screen went funny. It sort of flickered. Something came on then and I felt as if I'd been kicked in the stomach.

Mr. K.'s picture! It was a face . . . that goblin! It was that goblin Mr. K. had drawn that day I got spooked, and it was talking! That goblin-face was talking to us! "It's almost dark," it muttered in a low, growly voice, sneering at us. Slobbering, too. It was so gross. Then the screen went blank.

"Oh, man!" The words squeezed from my throat as we sprang up like jack-in-the-boxes, knocking our chairs backwards as we stumbled over each other to get away from the computer. Spencer stretched his arm out as far as he could without going too close to it again, and with his eyes scrunched shut, he snapped it off.

We crept backwards out of the studio, afraid to turn our backs on the computer screen, as if maybe the goblin could jump out. That damp, moldy odor drifted through the studio door with us as we stupidly pressed through together, shoulder to shoulder, neither of us wanting to be the last man out. Gasping for breath, we raced down the hall and dove into Spencer's room, slamming the door behind us.

On our way home from school through the playground the next day, Spence was shuffling through piles of leaves. "Ben—don't!" he shouted over his shoulder to me all of a sudden.

"Don't what?" I answered, surprised.

"What are you sticking me with?" he asked angrily.

It's Almost Dark

I was about to reply, "What are you talking about?" when I felt a sharp sting at my ankle. "Ouch!" We walked a little faster.

"Stop!" Spencer shouted. "Stop sticking me!"

"I'm not doing it!" I protested as we both broke into a run. "Ow!" Something stuck me again in the ankle.

Then we heard this growly voice behind us whisper, "It's almost dark!"

We freaked and looked behind us. There was nothing there. We ran then, ran all the way without stopping to Spencer's house. Even running, it seemed like it took forever to get there.

We streaked up the driveway. Breathless, we stumbled into the mudroom. Safe. We stood motionless for a second, panting, arms limp and dangling at our sides, just sort of staring sideways at each other. Then, both at the same time, we bolted for Mr. K.'s studio and peeked through the doorway. Mr. K. was feeding something into the scanner—something gruesome-looking. Instantly I was filled with dread. Spencer looked at me. I looked at him.

We both knew it at the same time. They were getting in. They were getting in from the scanner, the fancy new scanner Mr. K. had told us about! As insane as we knew it was, Mr. K. was scanning his creatures into the computer, out through the printer, and into the house! It felt as if I'd gulped down a golf ball of horror then, as I realized they were sliding out of the printer, onto the floor, into the house, and who knows where else?

Like lightning we charged down the hall toward Spencer's room. A sharp pain cut at my ankle again. Spencer was so freaked out, he slammed himself into his room before I got there.

"Spence! Spence!" I was rattling the door back and forth by the knob in a frenzy. "Let me in!" I fell in face first as he flung the door open.

Safe inside Spencer's room, we lay on our backs on the floor, exhausted, panting, shocked. We knew now it was the goblins who'd been grabbing at our ankles in the playground. I glanced over at the window and fear flooded into me as I remembered the goblin's scary words. *It's almost dark.* The day was over, and now it *was* dark.

I jumped straight up at the loud thumping on Spencer's door. "Spence? You in there?" It was Mr. K. I was both relieved and scared: relieved that a grown-up was nearby, and scared that it was dark and there were goblin-beings in the house and nobody knew it but us, and they were after us and how were we going to get rid of them, let alone tell Mr. K. that something had gone terribly wrong with his goblin book?

"Open up, Spence," Mr. K called again.

Spencer got up slowly, sort of like a zombie, his eyes looking like a dead guy's or something, his glasses hanging off one ear. He opened the door. Mr. K. came in. "Listen guys," he said. "Ben, how about a sleepover this weekend? Spence, your mom and I would like to go to a movie or whatever while you guys watch Shannon for a few hours Saturday night. What do you say?"

What could we say? "No, you can't leave us alone in the house, there are monsters in here and we're the only ones who can see them."

"Uh, sure, Dad. That's great," Spencer said, straightening his glasses. We were both in kind of a daze, bumping into each other, groping around for our stuff.

"Come on, Ben. It's dark. I'll drive you home. Spence, you can come, too."

"Do you have the cellular phone number, Spence?" Mr. K. called to us. He was pulling his jacket on. It was early Saturday evening. "You know you can reach us anytime that way." I was pretty impressed. Mr. K. always seems to have all kinds of state-of-the-art stuff to try out. I hoped we'd need to call him so we could play with the phone, but before long I was sorry I ever thought that.

The Kadisons left for the evening. Spence and I went into the studio to play a computer game, forgetting what had happened in there just a few days before. Big mistake. I began to smell that moldy smell. Was it my imagination or not? "Spence," I said calmly, not wanting to freak him out. "I'm smelling that stuff again."

"Uh-huh," he said vaguely, not taking his eyes off the screen. We were into that knights-of-the-Middle-Ages thing again. "What did you say?" He looked at me, then he looked at the screen again. "Look at this, Ben. This is so cool." In a moment we were back into the game, but I should have known from the smell that they were back ... and no one was home but us.

Suddenly there was a thud, and the whole house shook. Shannon screamed from her room. We shot from the studio like bullets. In seconds, the lights in the house flickered and went off. I groped through the hall, trying to find Spencer's room, feeling along the wall. I felt slimy stuff. "Stay with me, Spence!" I called to him over my shoulder.

"Ben! Ben!" There was another thud, then a dragging sound. "Ben!" Spencer called again. The smell was strong. Beardsley let out an awful howl. Had the goblins snatched him? I felt sick.

Fortunately some light was coming through the windows from the street. I found my way into Spencer's room and grabbed his flashlight and his hockey stick. I raced back out into the hall to find myself face-to-face with a moldy, smelly, steamy goblin! Being that close to him, it felt warm and damp, like at an indoor pool. The goblin was making growling, slobbering noises in his throat. I could have sworn he was laughing. "Ben!" The goblin had got hold of Spencer's leg! He'd been pulling him, and now he was dragging Spencer into the kitchen.

3

Shining Spencer's flashlight in front of me, I ran after them in time to see that Spencer had somehow managed to grab onto a kitchen chair.

FRIGHT TIME

He hung on like some kind of superhero with his face all squeezed tight, and the goblin kept yanking him, but Spencer hung on and dragged the chair right along with him across the kitchen floor till they got to the doorway of the dining room. Luckily by this time the kitchen chair had jammed sideways across the doorway. "Don't let go, Spence!" I yelled to him. "Don't let go!" I still had the hockey stick with me.

It was dark and I've never been so scared. By this time, I think Spencer was so incredibly freaked out, he couldn't even talk anymore, let alone shout. He was probably using up all his energy to hold on to the chair, anyway. That saved him. The goblin was still pulling on Spencer's legs, but because the chair was stuck, the goblin couldn't pull him through the doorway.

I raced around into the dining room with the flashlight and the hockey stick. I had to hold my breath, the goblin smelled so bad, giving off that weird steam and everything, but I had to do something, so I started whacking the goblin's knobby green knuckles with the hockey stick, and I kept on whacking. I couldn't stop, I was hitting him so hard.

It worked. It seemed as if I'd only hit him a

few times, but suddenly, he was gone! He sort of jumped backwards and disappeared into thin air, and the lights came on at the same time.

"Ben! I was so afraid he was gonna drag me all the way outside! And then what?" Spencer was sitting on the floor, rubbing his legs, looking around in a daze. He was fixing his hair, too—as if anybody were going to see him at that moment. It's funny, when I think of it now, but we weren't exactly laughing then.

Then we heard Shannon crying in her room. We ran in there to get her. She was okay. What a relief! We tucked her into her quilt, carried her into the living room, and set her up on the couch. We put one of her cartoon fairy-tales into the VCR. We sprawled out on the floor, but I couldn't keep my mind on Shannon's movie. I don't know how much time passed—maybe minutes, maybe an hour.

Then the lights began to flicker again. I shot straight up. Spencer was suddenly super-alert, terrified. We smelled mold. We looked at each other with dread.

"Call your dad—now!" I shouted, and we leaped to our feet.

Spencer fumbled for the cordless. "What's the

number?" he said to me, not realizing he was the one who had the number. He shuffled the papers on the coffee table, then grabbed the phone and started punching in the number. He gasped and dropped the phone, pulling his hands back as if the cordless had suddenly turned to hot coals. It hit the floor and bounced. He stared at me wide-eyed with fear.

"Spence!" I yelled, cold with panic. I picked up the phone. "What's the number!" I demanded. Then I froze with terror.

"Give us the girl," a growly voice sounded in the phone. I threw it down so fast, I didn't even see where it went.

It was our own screams we heard next, and we were still screaming when the lights went out again and we found ourselves on the floor, groping around for the flashlight which I somehow found, I don't know how. My hands were shaking so much I couldn't get it turned on, but when I finally did, all we could do was scream some more.

On the couch was the rumpled quilt we'd carried Shannon in—but she was gone!

When the lights came on I found Spencer standing in the mudroom, white as a ghost, staring at me as if he'd never been taught how to talk. His arm was raised. He was pointing to the outside door—the one that opens out onto the driveway and to the backyard. It was wide open.

We were paralyzed with panic. They'd taken Shannon out back! How would we find her in the woods? In the dark? I stuck my head out the door. Wait . . . I could hear her!

We grabbed our jackets from the pegs. I went back for the flashlight and the hockey stick and we charged outside, heading for the woods.

"I can hear her," Spencer said, panting.

"Keep talking to her, Spence," I told him. I swept the flashlight beam back and forth. Nothing. The smell was strong back there. At least that way we knew they were close, as disgusting as it was.

"It's getting dimmer, Ben," Spencer said very quietly.

"What, the flashlight?"

"No," he said. "Her voice. It's getting farther away." Then he got really quiet.

I strained to hear her. "It's swamp out there, Ben," he said.

I could tell he was scared. I was getting freaked, too.

We stopped again, and waited. We listened again. Spence looked at me. "I can't hear her any more. . . ."

4

I hadn't figured out how we were going to find our way into the woods, it was so dark.

"The jeep." Spencer looked at me like he was reading my mind or something. "The jeep," he said again, grabbing my shirtsleeve.

Now, Spence and I drive bumper cars—but his dad's jeep? "I don't know, Spence," I whined. "I don't know." I heard myself trailing off as I realized Spence had already streaked back into the house. I charged after him, catching up with him in the studio. He was rummaging around on top of Mr. K.'s desk.

"Yesss," Spencer hissed, raising something triumphantly in his hand. It was Mr. K.'s keys—the keys to his very new jeep. "You don't have to drive it too far," Spencer said, trying to reassure me.

"What?" I couldn't believe he was suggesting it. "I should drive? Why don't you drive? It's your dad's vehicle!"

It's Almost Dark

"Ben-n-n," he whined back at me, "you know I can't see over the wheel."

Great, I thought. This is just great. That's just what I need now, on top of everything else—to plow Mr. K.'s expensive new jeep into the bushes. "Go open the garage door," I told Spence. "Meet me out there." I went into the garage.

"Hurry up!" Spencer whispered loudly.

I got into Mr. K.'s jeep. I couldn't help thinking how cool it was to be behind the wheel of the thing, but I knew we'd be in for it if I put a scratch on it.

I stepped on the brake and shifted into drive. I got it out of the garage without too much trouble; luckily, Mr. K. had parked facing out! Spencer was sitting beside me. "Just go right across the backyard," he commanded, pushing his glasses up. It made me smile. "Hey," Spence complained. "What are you laughing about, anyway? My sister's out there."

I plowed the jeep through the backyard and straight toward the woods, hoping the Kadisons would someday forgive me if I left tire tracks across the lawn. We were bouncing, too—bigtime. This wasn't bumper cars—it was the real thing. We could have been killed!

I slammed on the brakes, practically hurling poor Spence through the windshield. Now I could see why he was so insistent about bringing the jeep out there. Its powerful headlights lit up the woods pretty far back, and sure enough, I saw steam, white and misty, not too far in the distance.

"See anything?" Spencer asked, squinting. I put the headlights up to high beam. We peered through the windshield into the woods, scanning the area, expecting to see Shannon—not what it was we really saw.

5

We kept looking through the windshield. Something was definitely moving. As the mist circled slowly in the headlight beams, we saw something step into the light. It was Shannon! On her own two feet, she walked calmly out of the shadows, shielding her eyes from the brightness of the headlights.

Relief turned fast into panic. "Oh, Ben, what are we supposed to do now?" Spencer was gripping my arm, and I was gripping the steering wheel.

"Grab her!" I blurted out impulsively. Instantly we both jumped down from the jeep. I'd left the headlights on high beam. We both plunged into the bushes as if we knew exactly what we were doing. I ran toward Shannon and scooped her up in my arms.

I got Shannon into the jeep. She was smiling at me. She wasn't hurt!

"Ben!" Spencer was still outside. He pointed out into the woods. "Get out here! Something's moving!" There was an old blanket in the car, and I grabbed that and ran toward Spencer. I threw the blanket at him. "Go!" I shouted.

Spence plunged into the bushes like I've never seen him run. It was pretty heroic actually, but he's kind of clumsy. First thing he did was trip over a log. He struggled to his feet, though, and plunged deeper into the woods, straight to where he'd seen something moving. I followed right behind him with the hockey stick, ready to bash some more goblins.

Running with the blanket, Spence took a flying leap and tented it over the thing in one fast move, throwing his whole body over the squirming bundle.

"I got it!" he shouted in my direction. "Ben! I can't hold him! Help!"

I raced over to him and threw myself on top of him and the thing he'd just captured. Whatever it was quieted down after jerking around under there a little longer.

"What exactly are you planning to do with it now?" Spence asked me, pressing down harder on the bundle with his body to keep the thing still.

"Well, what is it, first of all, pea-brain?" I asked. "I don't know what to do with it till you tell me what it is!" The bundle twitched.

"It's a goblin, you idiot!" he said. "It's one of them!" Then his voice quieted down a little. "I think it's a baby."

"No way."

"Way! I'm telling you, Ben. I think it's a baby one." He felt a corner of the blanket. Holding my breath, I slowly lifted up another corner to see what was underneath, then snapped it back down really fast.

"I'm afraid to look."

"I can't believe you, Ben!" Spencer said. "You just drove the jeep! You got the goblin to let go of my legs! Now you're gonna wimp out on me?"

"Am not."

"Are too." Spencer casually leaned back on one elbow, still holding down the bundle with the rest of his body.

"You're not thinking of bringing it with us, are you?" I said. He said nothing, getting me totally frustrated. "Are you?"

I don't know how I got the jeep back into the garage. At least it wasn't hard to get Shannon back to bed. Then I began to worry. "Spence," I said, "what are we going to tell your dad about the jeep?"

"I put back the keys. Piece of cake. He'll never know," he said.

Then the printer started running by itself in the studio. A goblin-face slid out! He was showing big, ratty-looking teeth. "Why won't they leave us alone?" I yelled. Then the phone rang! Spencer dove out of the studio, he was so startled. "You better not lock me out of your room!" I called after him. "Answer the phone!"

"You!" he shouted. Great. This time he'd locked himself in the bathroom.

The phone was still ringing. I was afraid to

91

answer it, afraid not to. Somehow, I knew it wasn't going to be Mr. K., and it probably wasn't my mom, either. I'd already called her and said everything was okay. Yeah, right. That was before goblin-time.

The cordless was still on the floor where I'd thrown it earlier. I picked it up, held it near my ear.

"Give him back!" came the now-familiar growl.

Fear crawled up my neck. I looked around. Everything was silent. Why hadn't Spence come out of the bathroom? I looked at the cordless. I could still hear funny sounds coming from it. I don't know why, but something came over me. Either that or I'm just a complete idiot. I guess I was beginning to get angry.

I picked up the cordless and shouted, "Come and get him!"

6

Now you've done it, I told myself. I went to the bathroom door and put my ear up against it, wondering if Spencer had fallen asleep in there.

92

It's Almost Dark

"Spence?" I called.

"Yeah?"

"Are you coming out, or what?"

"Did you answer the phone?"

"Oh, I answered the phone, all right," I told him.

Spencer opened the door. "Ben," he said, looking at me gravely, "my glasses are out there. Now I'll have to wear the nerdy ones."

"That's not quite major," I said. "Listen, that was them on the phone just now."

Spencer knew I meant the goblins. He moaned. "We've got to get the baby one in here before my parents get back."

We dragged the bundle in and set it down on the floor of the mudroom. Immediately Beardsley began to spit at it. Not a good sign. "I don't know about this," I said.

"Let me out," it croaked. Spence was right. It was a baby goblin.

"You're not going to like this, Spence," I said. "When the goblins called on the phone," I confessed, "well, I told them to come and get him."

"What?" he screeched. "That's great, Ben. Maybe they'll drag me around the house some more, or suffocate us or something! Maybe

FRIGHT TIME

they'll grab us around the throat and squeeze till our eyes pop out and . . ." He was totally wound up!

"All right, all right!" I shouted. "Calm down! We need to figure out what to do!"

"We'll hide him in my closet, that's what we'll do," Spencer said.

"That's no solution!" I said. "They'll be coming for him!"

We dragged the baby goblin down the hall and into Spencer's room. "As if there's any room for him in my closet," Spencer griped. Surprisingly enough, the goblin let us set him up in the closet. He immediately fell asleep.

We collapsed on the beds. What would my mom think if she knew there were goblins in the Kadisons' house and they were moldy and smelly and disgusting with ratty-looking teeth and they were grabbing us and dragging us around and kidnapping Spencer's sister? And that we had a baby one in the closet? This was getting to be an awfully long night so far—and it wasn't even half over.

Spencer and I had some major planning to do—like how were we going to get the baby goblin back out of the house again? I was getting really scared that the other goblins would come after us—come back in the house to get the baby and terrorize us big-time. I started blaming myself. I had to open up my big mouth and tell them, "Come and get him!"

"Spence? You awake?" I said after a while. The light was still on.

"I don't see how I could not be awake—after all, that thing is making such a racket in there," he complained.

"This isn't working. We need to get him out of the closet," I said, thinking Spence would probably go lock himself in another room and make me do it. I was beginning to smell goblin now, too, and it wasn't coming from the baby. And I was afraid to get Spencer alarmed. Any minute now he could get all wound up again.

Yes, I was definitely smelling goblin again! I knew it. They were there! I just didn't know where. They were probably trying to find their baby. It was like the goblin said, in the light, we couldn't see them. That meant the lights might go off again any time now! You can't imagine how freaky it was when that smell was in the air. It meant only one thing: Something was going to happen . . . soon.

7

Spence and I opened the closet door very carefully. It was quiet in there now. Beardsley was right at our feet. He wanted to get at that goblin, like it was one big mouse.

Spencer sat down on the bed. In the dim lamplight, his face looked shadowy. I sat down on the other bed. "Do you think he fell asleep in there?" Spence asked me.

I sighed. "This is getting so ridiculous," I answered. "Is this a dream, or what?"

"If it is," he said, "I hope I wake up soon." Spencer dove down onto his bed and covered his head with his pillow.

I edged over to the closet and looked inside. I looked again. "Uh, Spence," I said. "There's a problem."

There was no baby goblin in the closet! The little creature had left the old blanket we'd wrapped him in and disappeared! We didn't even know how long he'd been missing.

He had to be in the house somewhere. "You know this place better than I do, Spence," I said. "If you were a baby goblin—"

It's Almost Dark

"Where would I hide?" Spencer cut in. "I don't know. Maybe we should follow the odor."

"But the baby doesn't smell that much," I started to say, then remembered I'd been smelling goblin. They were around somewhere, and now, in the middle of the night, everything was quiet. A good time for a goblin to jump out and pull you down. I swallowed my usual ball of fear. "Bring the flashlight," I said to Spencer. "And the hockey stick. The baby's got to be here somewhere."

Our first stop was the studio. The printer kicked on, and as usual I jumped. I was so whacked out with fear. It seemed the goblins could turn on the printer whenever they felt like it—which also meant that more goblins could keep getting in! I shivered.

I thought I'd go nuts anytime now. Yes, I was going to lose my mind altogether. I was going to end up a crazy person who told stories about goblins dragging him around the house. My mind was speeding with awful thoughts when suddenly Beardsley let out one of those cat howls the way cats do when they're fighting with each other. But there was only one cat in this house. "Spence? Spence, where are you?" I called. I freaked out. The smell of goblin was thick and right near me. Spencer was suddenly nowhere to be seen, and he had the flashlight and the hockey stick.

A second later I thought for sure my life was over! Before I knew what hit me, a thick tent came down over my head—something rough and scratchy—that old blanket from the car! Instantly I was wrapped tight in stuffy darkness. I could hardly breathe! "Spence!" I yelled, hearing my own voice muffled by the heavy cloth. "Spence, quit it! Get this thing off me!"

Nothing that we'd gone through so far terrified me this much. I struggled and squirmed, only to realize that my arms were clamped down against my sides. I couldn't even move them. This couldn't be Spencer. He'd never be this mean, and whatever was holding me was much stronger than either one of us.

"Ben!" It was Spencer calling me, half whispering, not wanting to wake Shannon. Now I knew it wasn't Spencer who had trapped me inside the blanket. But if it wasn't Spencer—who was it?

I was desperate with panic. I could hardly breathe, let alone scream, though I'm sure I was screaming. I might as well have been drowning in the ocean.

"Spence! Help me! Get me out!" I managed to call to him, but I didn't know if he heard me. Once again waves of panic surged through me as I realized that my blanket-trap was moving. I was being dragged! Something was dragging me, bumping me against things, hauling me through the house and through the garage and out onto the driveway!

Then I felt grass under me. It had to be the goblins. They were dragging me across the backyard and out to where I knew it would be very hard to find me! I must have passed out then. Everything just went blank.

I no longer knew if it was day or night when I woke up. I didn't even know how long I'd been gone, or where I was. What day was this? There was no way of knowing. I blinked my eyes, and to my horror I realized I still couldn't move my arms. It seemed I was still wrapped in the blanket—a captive. The goblins had wrapped me in the blanket with my arms pinned against my sides. At least my head was sticking out. At least I could breathe. At least I could see something.

FRIGHT TIME

It might have been daytime now, or maybe not. There was a little light—maybe from the floodlights—coming in from some opening to wherever it was I was . . . hanging! "This can't be happening!" I moaned out loud. The goblins had hung my blanket up. I was hanging inside a tree!

It was impossible to believe, but then, it seemed that anything was possible once you got the point, whatever Mr. Kadison put into his picturebook could happen to you right then and there, now that the goblins had found their way into the human world! Our world! I clenched my teeth together so hard I thought they'd crack.

I twisted my head sideways, trying to figure out for sure if this was the inside of a tree or if I was really crazy.

I yelled, choking with disgust at something squirming, clinging to the wall—if you could call it a wall, all twisted branches and twigs and roots and vines and mossy stuff, like the stuff that stuck to the goblins. Something big and brown and slimy-looking was wiggling near my face. I felt like a wimp then, whining when I saw something so totally gross that you wouldn't want to touch . . . something you definitely wouldn't want to drop onto you from the ceiling.

Then I looked up. They were all over the place! Big shiny brown slimy squirming centipedes or something. Bugs! Bugs with millions of squiggling legs, and they were all moving toward me!

"Help!" I screamed. Please, somebody hear me. . . .

I think I kept falling asleep and waking up, but I have no idea how long I hung there in the blanket. It seemed like days. My lips began to dry out. I began to worry how I'd get water. I knew a person can't live too long without water. I wondered if my mom and dad would begin to wonder why I didn't show up at home. It didn't seem like anybody could hear me screaming.

"Help!" I yelled some more.

I was afraid to look at the walls again, or up above my head. It was thick and stringy with twisted vines and bark, and alive with that mass of crawling bugs! Moldy goblin-smelling moss hung disgustingly close to my face. If there really is a hell, I thought, feeling sorry for myself, this is definitely it.

"Somebody! Anybody! I'm in here—inside the big tree in the middle! Help!"

It's no use, I thought then, feeling sure I was doomed. I'm a dead man. No one can hear me.

Then I heard footsteps outside, dry and crunchy like in the woods. I was flooded with relief. Saved! Someone was coming through the opening. Yes! This nightmare is officially over!

No! Not yet! A goblin stomped up to me and loomed right up close to my face, hovering over me, damp and stinking, growling and showing his pointed ratty teeth.

The goblin began to unhook my blanket.

"Let me go!" I demanded. I struggled, thinking I might be able to escape from him. No such luck. He held on to me with a grip that was stronger than any dad's I know of.

I was chilled with cold fright. He was dragging me somewhere. I was being rolled and slammed face-first into damp earth. Then I realized we weren't going toward the opening. He was dragging me deeper, deeper into the monster tree! How big could the inside of a tree be?

Spitting out pieces of dirt as my face scraped the ground, I realized, to my horror, that this was no ordinary tree. This was where they lived! Was here where they had taken Shannon, this horrid, damp place of twisted roots, stringy moss, squirming bugs? Had Mr. K. thought up a place so horrible, creatures so hideous, and then written it all into his book? Was Mr. K.'s imagination this twisted?

Suddenly we stopped moving. I opened my eyes. We must have gone deep down into the earth, because this sure wasn't the inside of a tree anymore. This was like a cave—a dirt cave—and you could see parts of really old tree roots sticking out of the dirt walls. I didn't want to see it or them, but there they were, a whole big bunch of them, a whole bunch of goblins— baby ones, too. The smell alone nearly killed me for good.

Suddenly my arms were free. I sat up and yanked the blanket off me, struggling to make it to my feet. I was wobbly, but I managed to stand. The big goblin who was dragging me stuck his face near mine. He pointed to something. "You're next... " he said to me.

"Leave me alone, you big fat disgusting slob!" I shouted back at him. I started swinging at him, punching him, kicking him, but another goblin grabbed me from behind.

"Let go of me!" I screamed. "Let me out of here! You can't keep me down here! You're not even real!" I kicked my legs wildly, trying to free myself from their grip. Two more goblins twisted my arms behind my back. Each time I kicked and struggled, they tightened their hold on me. I couldn't move.

They pulled me over to where the big one was pointing. "You're next," he growled again, and I looked closer. It was a cage—a cage made out of twisted branches and dead tree roots, tied shut with pieces of old, frayed rope the goblins must have stolen from people's backyards. If only Mr. Kadison knew what he had unleashed in the neighborhood!

I would have fallen down if the goblins hadn't been holding me up. What was lying on the floor of the cage made me sick with fright. It was someone's jacket. I was sure it looked familiar. I could have sworn it was my friend Greg's, or maybe Jeremy's from around the corner. Were they torturing these other kids, too? They had to be stopped . . . but how?

I wasn't ready for the shock that hit me then. There were bones scattered around the floor of the cage, too. Bones! They're going to eat me! My mind screamed in terror. How many times could a guy be almost a dead man in one day? I was next!

I looked around the cave in a frenzy. I had to figure out how to escape from them. This wasn't funny any more—this was life and death—*my* life and death!

They had candles burning, and it dawned on me that they had brought some of Mrs. K.'s candles down there, and someone's kerosene lantern. I had to get away. I knew I'd better start thinking—double-time.

But it was too late for thinking. Before I knew it, they'd shoved me into the tree-root cage and tied me in! I gripped the twisted cage bars and shook the cage. "Let me out of here!" I demanded. "You can't keep me in here! Someone's going to find out and kill you all. You just wait!" I screamed.

"*You're next . . .*" one of them said again. I was beginning to think they really didn't have that many things they could say. I don't even know how they learned how to talk at all—but then, whatever Mr. K. wrote about them, I guess they could do.

"*You're next . . .*" they taunted me.

FRIGHT TIME

"I screamed and screamed, knowing it wasn't going to make any difference. Who was going to hear me all the way down here?

It was torture! I covered my ears. I squeezed my eyes shut. Then I opened them. Then real fast I shut them again! Some goblins had started shuffling toward the cage, shuffling closer to me with their arms stretched out like ghouls—like zombies—making "Urrrrr" noises at me, staring at me, closing in on the cage, closer and closer!

They were crowding around the cage now, all around me. "Get away from me!" I shrieked. I was petrified. They were sticking their arms in through the bars, all the way up to their shoulders, waving them back and forth at me, reaching in at me, clutching at me with those warty green clawlike hands!

"Urrrrr!" They were baring their ugly teeth at me, slobbering, snapping at me! I backed away from them, pressing myself against the back of the cage. I covered my ears again. Their growly, gurgling noises were so disgusting!

"Help!" I yelled, hoping maybe this time somebody was going to hear me.

"Ben!"

"What was that? A voice!

"Ben!" It was Spencer! I almost thought I was dreaming. No one had come to find me for so long, I'd figured that it was the end of me.

"Ben! Are you okay?"

"Spence!" I shouted. "Down here! Go into the tree!"

I couldn't believe it, but there was Spencer. I couldn't understand how he'd found his way out here to this tree. How did he know how to find it? He was stepping carefully down into the dirt cave, and he was dragging a bundle behind him.

"Ben! I've been looking everywhere! Come on!" he chattered on. "Ben, look! I found the baby!" He'd been dragging the baby goblin with him!

"Spence! Take him back outside!" I blurted out. "Take him back out!"

"But, Ben," he protested. "Why? What do you mean, take him back out? I came to get you! He led me here! He told me right where to go, too!"

"Unwrap him, Spence!" I shouted. Spencer

had dragged the baby goblin here in a blanket. "Show them the baby! Then take him back outside! They'll follow you out!"

Spencer had lugged the hockey stick and an aluminum baseball bat along with the goblin bundle. Smart move, I said silently. We'll bash the heck out of them! I knew that once the goblins saw the baby, they'd follow Spencer back outside.

But how was I going to get out of the cage? Getting the goblins to leave me alone and go after the baby was my only chance to escape. It would be kind of like a hostage exchange. Spencer could give back the baby in exchange for me!

Spencer started lugging the baby back out, along with the equipment he'd brought. What a guy, I thought. "Drop the sticks, Spence!" I shouted. "Just get out with the baby!"

Quickly I looked around to see if I could free myself from the cage. The candles! Mrs. K., you're a lifesaver, I thought. I was able to reach one of her "borrowed" candles by extending my arm as far as I could through the cage.

I can't believe these dumb mutants haven't burned themselves up in here, with all these candles going, I thought, holding the candle flame next to the ratty old rope the goblins had used to tie the cage shut.

My idea worked! I burned through the rope and burst out of the cage, scrambling up the rooty pathway from the cave toward the tree opening. I scooped up the hockey stick and the baseball bat and charged outside.

"Spence!" I called, just in time to see a bunch of goblins closing in on him. "Drop the baby! Take the bat!"

I tossed the bat over toward him. The confusion of the goblins was definitely in our favor. None of the goblins seemed to know what to do next, and luckily for us, the baby started wandering away!

"Urrrr...." Now some of the goblins started trudging after the baby. Spence and I started swinging like crazy! We were clobbering everything in sight. It's a good thing we didn't maul each other that day!

"Look out, Spence!" I yelled. "There's one behind you!"

Spencer whirled around with the bat like a ninja, whacking a goblin clear off the ground, into the air!

Then, all of a sudden, I realized every time we

clobbered a goblin, it disappeared! They sure had some sort of weird talent for disappearing— they did it all the time! I mean, we were destroying them, but there was no blood or guts or anything! They were just gone.

It wasn't long before we had cleared the area enough to make a getaway. Whatever goblins were left began heading further back into the woods. We ran like anything. Right away, Spence fell. "Look, Ben!" he called, his face to the ground. "My glasses! Right where I dropped them!" He put them on. "Yesss," he said contentedly as he sat up and pocketed the nerdy pair. "Now I don't have to go back to school looking like a dork."

"You're already a dork," I told him, punching his arm.

We got back to the house. We were exhausted. We got some of Mrs. K's huge glasses and filled them with ice and water. We must have slugged down icewater for five minutes straight.

"Hey, Spence?" I asked him, "What day is this, anyway?"

"It's still Saturday night, man," he answered, looking at me strangely. "Is this the worst night of your life, or what?" he asked me. "It is, for me."

Saturday night? "Spence! Are you trying to

tell me I was out there only tonight? It felt like I was their prisoner for days!"

"Well... yeah, Ben. Tonight. Now. Saturday night," he said. Then his face turned very serious. "Ben— while you were trapped in the tree—they almost got me for good. I almost didn't make it back out there to find you." Then Spencer told me some stuff that was pretty horrible.

"I was looking all over the house for the baby goblin," he told me. "All of a sudden one of them was on top of me! He got his big disgusting arms around me and I couldn't move. Ben, he was slobbering all over me! Just like the Wilsons' dog! It was so gross!

"The smell was really strong, too. I was so scared, I could hardly make any noise, or scream or anything. Then he threw me down and started pulling me by my feet!"

I felt my mouth go dry. "Then what?"

"Then he dragged me into my room. Luckily I managed to grab my flashlight when he pulled me near the bed. I wanted to shine it in his eyes and bash him on the head with it, too. But then he grabbed my throat!"

Spencer told me the goblin had growled, "You're coming with me...."

FRIGHT TIME

"It was horrible, Ben! I couldn't breathe! But then I got the flashlight turned on and I shot the light right into his face. He dropped me when the light surprised him! Then I jumped up and grabbed the hockey stick and whammed him, just as we did out back!"

"Did he disappear?"

"Yup. Just as they always do. Oh man, Ben— I can't take this."

Goblin-time. It was like no time I'd ever been through before. It was enough to make anybody crazy. Of course, the Kadisons are so nutty to begin with, it was almost as if Spencer expected stuff like that to happen! Not me. I hoped I'd never see anything like this again as long as I live. As far as I was concerned, I'd been awfully close to being a dead guy just a few hours ago.

We put in a computer game and sat motionless in front of the screen. We were both totally wiped, but it was still Saturday night, and we were still in charge till Mr. and Mrs. K. got home.

After a few minutes the game flickered and went off, and my stomach lurched. Something I definitely did not want to see appeared on the computer screen. A big goblin face. My brain was already working overtime. I passed out cold on the floor.

10

I don't know how long I lay on the floor. The Kadisons still hadn't come home. We were both beginning to wonder what was taking them so long. I would have felt pretty stupid lying on the floor if they'd come home just then.

"Is he gone?" I said to Spence.

"He's gone, Ben," Spencer said. Spence wasn't smiling. While we were playing the game, that big goblin face had taunted us from the computer screen.

"Did you hear what he said?" I whimpered. I was still lying on the floor. Spence sat beside me. "He said they'll come for all of us next time, Spence! That could be tonight!"

"They'll keep coming back," Spencer said. "I wish my parents would hurry up and get home! The goblins will keep torturing us unless we, uh, undo them, you know, like, erase them. All of them."

"What are you saying, Spence? Stuff the goblins back into the computer? Shove them back through the scanner? They won't fit!"

"Well," he answered, "I was thinking, like, get rid of them with something else my dad made up. Like Tarx. Look at all the cool gear he has! We could blow them away if we had all that neat equipment! If the goblins can get out, why not Tarx?"

I couldn't argue with Spencer. In just a couple of days, I was finding out exactly how smart he really is.

We didn't have much time to plan how we were going to get rid of the goblins.

"Let's do it *now*. We have to do it now! We can't spend the rest of the night with *goblins* chasing us around the house," Spencer said.

"Not to mention losing your baby sister. Or getting kidnapped again!"

"Here's a picture of Tarx!" Spencer said, sorting through Mr. K.'s pictures.

"No good, Spence," I told him. "That one's on a board. We need something on plain paper, something we can feed into the scanner."

"Look at him, Ben," Spence said, holding up the full-length portrait of the futuristic superhero. "Awesome, isn't he?"

"Outrageous," I agreed.

Luckily, Spencer found a copy of Tarx on paper so he could scan him into the computer. He fed the picture through the scanner. "Here's hoping," he told me. "Get ready."

I crossed my fingers behind my back.

I don't remember exactly how it happened. Spence doesn't either. So many creepy and mysterious things happened in the Kadison house that night, so many crazy things appearing and disappearing. All we remember is that Tarx was suddenly just . . . there!

It's a good thing the Kadisons' big old house has high ceilings. Tarx was eight feet tall! "Ben, meet Tarx," Spencer said breathlessly, staring up at this giant. Spence pushed his glasses up.

I wasn't exactly sure I wanted to shake hands with Tarx. I wasn't even sure how you're supposed to talk to a cyberbeing.

"Uh, hi," I said stupidly. Then I got my head straight. "Tarx, you must help us."

We told Tarx about the goblins, and that we had to get rid of them—fast.

"What does Tarx mean, anyway?" Spencer asked.

Tarx had a booming voice, just as you'd imagine him to have. Of course, Mr. K. had created him that way. "Tarx means Technically Advanced Robotic Exo-titans," he told us.

"Yesss!" Spence grinned at me excitedly.

"How many of your warriors can we bring here?" I asked. "We have to blast these goblins now!"

Spence was already back at the computer. "Tarx, who do you want to bring out of cyberspace? I'm ready to print them out right now."

"XT-2 and XT-7 are available," Tarx said in his booming voice. "We'll have plenty of firepower."

Firepower? That got me nervous. I started to say something, but I didn't have to.

"We'll be carrying out our mission where they're hiding," Tarx said, reading my mind. "Spencer tells me the goblins can be found inside a tree out back."

Then, just as suddenly as Tarx had arrived, two more cyberwarriors were standing in the studio, scanned in by Spence. It was time to waste goblins.

Spence and I went for our usual stuff, the flashlight, the hockey stick, and the bat. Actually we felt kind of stupid with those little things, compared to fireballs, laser power, and night-vision visors. This was intense. With their night-vision visors, Tarx and the XTs would be able to see where the goblins were lurking. I was psyched. We were fed up with goblin-time. We just wanted things to get back to normal.

We decided XT-2 would guard Shannon during the mission. He stood on the inside of her doorway like an eight-foot-tall wooden soldier. He didn't budge.

"Now lead us to the tree," Tarx commanded. I guess he's used to commanding everybody. The flashlight and the backyard floodlights were enough light for us, and Tarx could see everything in the dark anyway.

We found the tree and waited a moment. "Now what?" Spence asked. He pushed at his glasses. I stood close to the opening of the tree. There was a little dim light coming from it. Gross! There were goblins down there. I could smell the moldy odor coming up. I covered my face. I couldn't stand the odor, or remembering being trapped down there with them.

Tarx launched some sort of pellet into the opening.

"What's that?" Spence asked.

"Just a smoke pellet," Tarx answered. "To

bring them out."

We moved back and waited. Soon, some of the biggest, ugliest, smelliest ones began to come out of the tree opening. Tarx raised his right arm and pointed it at the goblins. A big, flaming fireball burst from Tarx's arm!

We gasped.

I couldn't believe what happened then. The fireball surrounded the goblins for a split-second. Then it flamed out and disappeared! The goblins weren't dead, though. They were coming at us! The smell this time was more gross than ever. It was totally putrid!

The goblins were melting and shrieking! Their eyes were—and this freaked me out—dissolving and pouring out of their faces! They were coming at us, holding their dripping, steaming arms out in front of them, like the worst monster movie that ever kept you awake after you saw it! The smell was unbelieveable, and their big, rats' teeth—suddenly they were dropping onto the ground!

More and more goblins started coming out of the tree.

"When are they going to *stop!*" Spencer shrieked. He was holding both arms over his face. It was so gross!

Tarx and XT-7 raised their laser devices and started vaporizing the goblins as they came out. There was so much choking, foul-smelling goblin-smoke, we thought we were probably going to suffocate!

We screamed and ran behind another tree. I covered my eyes. Spence had jumped behind me and was gripping me tight—almost as tight as the goblins had. It was terrifying. Even with my eyes covered I couldn't get the horrible sight of their melting faces out of my brain.

Then Tarx went over to the tree and launched one big fireball into the opening. The rest of Mr. K.'s nightmarish creatures got totally vaporized down inside their dirt cave. The stench of it all was like the worst toxic-waste dump you could imagine. You couldn't breathe from the fumes!

Then everything got quiet. I couldn't believe not a single neighbor noticed the flames or the smell. It was as if we were the only ones who saw it all. I wasn't sure. To this day, Spencer's parents don't know what went on that night, and it was their house! It was dark in the woods again, except for the light coming through from Spencer's backyard. The air was thick with the foul-smelling smoke that slowly swirled between the trees.

Spencer and I came out from our hiding place. "How will you get back into cyberspace, Tarx?" Spencer asked him.

"The XTs and I can leave your world whenever we wish," Tarx told us in his booming voice. I almost told him to keep it down, but I kept quiet, hoping no neighbors would hear him. Besides, I wasn't ready to start ordering this guy around!

"We'll be able to get back faster if you boys send our pictures back through the scanner," Tarx went on, "but we don't have to remain among you humans unless we choose to."

I didn't know if that made me feel better or worse. That meant the goblins had enjoyed staying with us and tormenting us! Ugh! "So the goblins wanted to be here?" I asked.

"They enjoy causing as much trouble as they can," Tarx said. "Spencer, your father created them that way. If we see any more of them on the inside," he told us, "we'll take care of them. They won't be back, not these creatures, anyway."

What did he mean by that? Did that mean there could be other stuff coming out of Mr. K.'s weird imagination? The very idea of it made me sick to my stomach!

Then Tarx and XT-7 were just . . . gone.

We streaked back into the house. XT-2 was gone, too, and Shannon was fast asleep. She'd never even heard what was going on! We went into the studio and found some photocopies of Tarx and the XTs. We scanned them in, just to make sure. "Let's hide this picture of Tarx in my room," Spencer suggested, "in case we ever need him again."

Just then we felt a rumble along the floor. The garage door was going up. "They're home!" Spencer said. We raced in circles around the studio for a few seconds, knocking into each other, not knowing what to do first.

"Act normal!" Spence shouted.

We dashed to Spencer's room to make it look as if we were just hanging out. I lay back on the bed and toyed with Spencer's baseball mitt. Spencer jumped onto the other bed and started playing his guitar. We made some silly conversation so his mom and dad would hear us and think everything was the same as usual.

"Spence? We're home!" Mr. K. sang out, poking his head into Spencer's doorway. He always raises his eyebrows and smiles a big, broad smile as if he's about to jump out, open his arms real wide and yell, "It's showtime!" Except, in the Kadison household, it's always showtime.

Mr. K. stretched, yawned, and took off his jacket. "Looks like you guys did all right," he said, grinning. He scrubbed Spencer's hair with his hand. "You tired, big guy?"

"Uh...no. Me? I'm not tired," Spencer fudged, poking at his glasses.

Mrs. K. came in then. "These guys ought to get to bed, Dan," she said. "It's getting awfully late. Ben, what would your mom think if she knew I let you stay up so late?"

"Mommy!" It was Shannon!

Oh, no, I said to myself. Spencer and I stood up, pretending not to notice that she had just come into Spencer's room. Mrs. K. quickly scooped Shannon up in her arms. She looked at us very suspiciously.

"How did she get so messed up, Spencer?" Mrs. K. asked Spence as she smoothed Shannon's hair with her free hand. "What have you been up to, honey?" she asked Shannon, cuddling her, fussing over her, the way moms do. "Spencer, I told you—no roughhousing with the baby!" She was already on her way to Shannon's room to put her back to bed.

"I had a bad dream about monsters," we heard Shannon telling Mrs. K. We just looked at each other as Spence pushed his glasses up again.

"Don't worry, guys," Mr. K. told us. "Our Shannon seems to have quite an imagination. Takes after me!" He laughed. "C'mon. Let's get some sleep, fellas. Looks like it's all quiet around here."

At least, I thought so—for a while. Recently, Mr. Kadison called us into the studio to show us the new book he's working on. He held up a picture of the newest character he's created. "So guys, what do you think of this one?" he asked cheerfully, grinning his usual grin. He's totally clueless.

What I saw made me feel like I was going to be sick right there in the middle of the studio. My legs began to feel wobbly. Spencer got that oh, no expression on his face.

We looked at each other, each knowing what the other one was thinking.

FRIGHT TIME

Mr. K. was already scanning the picture into the computer!

His new book—it's going to be about ghosts. . . .

Scary Harry

by Terry Patrick

1

I'm not sure when my older brother, Harry, started acting strange, but I think it all began on the night before we moved to Parkville.

Every time the wind blew, the shadows shook and the leaves rustled as if they were sighing. I wasn't looking forward to moving again.

Mom and Dad were talking quietly. "Barnaby just wants to let the boys know that he thinks of them, Margie! I'm sure they'll love what he sent them."

Uncle Barnaby! Dad's older brother. Uncle

Fright Time

Barnaby is an importer. He's always traveling around the world, going to strange places and buying cool stuff. Dad said that Uncle Barnaby even has a real human shrunken head! Sometimes, he and Dad meet up, and Uncle Barnaby gives stuff to Dad to give to us. The last time, he gave Harry a telescope and I got the jaw of a shark.

Harry must have been listening, too, because we crashed into each other running down the stairs. By the time Dad pushed the swinging kitchen door open, we were waiting for him.

"Why am I not surprised to find you guys here?" he asked.

He pulled out a long tube about as thick as my arm and as long as my leg and handed it to me. It was heavy.

"From Uncle Barnaby," said Dad.

The card read, "For Christmas, your birthday, Halloween, and whatever else I missed. Love, UB."

I opened it up, and couldn't believe my eyes— a real samurai sword! Okay, so I was a Ninja nut a few years ago. But this was the real thing.

"Now, Jesse," said Mom, "you must be very careful with that. It's not a toy."

"Okay, Mom." I held it in my hands. It was very heavy. I pulled the sword out of the scabbard very slowly. It was the neatest thing I had ever held.

"Barnaby, wherever you are," said Mom, rolling her eyes. Then to me, she said, "You be real careful with it, Jesse."

Dad nodded his head in agreement. "It's for display purposes only."

"Sure, Dad."

All this time, of course, Harry was standing by the side of the table, trying really hard to look like he was NOT waiting to see what Barnaby had sent home with Dad for him. There was no way in the world that he would ask Dad what he got for him.

Dad put his bag down and opened it. He took out a small square box.

"This is for you, Harry," he said.

Dad held the package out. Harry took it, still Mr. Cool. He shook it and peeled the paper away just a tiny bit, then folded it back quickly. I didn't even get a chance to see what it was.

"Thanks, Dad," he said. He turned and walked out of the kitchen real fast and raced up the stairs.

"Don't thank me, Harry," Dad called after him. "Thank Uncle Barnaby."

"Hey, do you know what he got?" I asked Dad.

"No, Jesse," said Dad. "Barnaby wouldn't tell me. He said it was between him and Harry."

I said good-night to Mom and Dad, and ran upstairs.

"Jesse," Mom shouted, "Don't run with a sword in your hand!"

I slowed to a walk and stopped outside Harry's door.

"Harry?"

"Go away, Jesse! Beat it! It's past your bedtime," he said.

"Creep!" I shouted back.

I walked slowly on to my room, closed the door, and shut off the light. I listened for a minute to see if Mom or Dad was coming upstairs. When I was sure they weren't, I pulled the sword out of the scabbard and held it up to the moonlight.

Then I noticed something strange. Carved into the blade and handle of the sword were these weird little monkey skeletons. They were all fighting each other. One monkey was chopping off another monkey's head. Another monkey was pulling off his enemy's arm. Two other monkeys seemed to be strangling each other. It was really gross.

I slid the sword back into the scabbard and hung it on the edge of my bed.

I lay down on top of the covers and stretched out with my hands behind my head, watching the moon shadows dance on the wall.

What if Uncle Barnaby gave Harry the shrunken head? One thing about Uncle Barnaby, you never could tell what he was going to do. If he had given Harry the shrunken head, that could be why Harry wouldn't let anyone see his present. Mom would be grossed out for sure. I bet Dad would want Harry to return it...to Uncle Barnaby, I mean.

Harry could show it to me, though. I would never rat on him, no matter what. We may be brothers, but he's the best friend I ever had. Why was he acting so strange all of a sudden?

I looked around my room and suddenly found myself staring at my feet. Maybe it was those monkeys on the sword, but suddenly I couldn't get over how much my feet looked like hands.

FRIGHT TIME

You have your big toe, which is like your thumb, then four other toes like your four other fingers.

I don't know why I did it, but I suddenly sat up and pulled out the sword to look at the monkey carvings again. It was really strange. You couldn't tell a monkey foot from a monkey hand.

Then it hit me. It wasn't that my feet looked like human hands. They looked like monkey hands.

I put the sword back and lay down again. Weird, every time I looked at my feet, they looked more and more like monkey hands. It got so bad, I finally put a pillow over them. Only then was I able to fall asleep.

Later that night, I woke up and heard a dog barking somewhere. Dogs almost never barked in this neighborhood. Then I thought that I smelled something awful in the air.

"Burnt hair," I whispered to myself.

Fortunately, the smell went away quickly. Then I thought I heard a really weird buzzing noise that just went on and on.

I don't know when I fell back asleep, but the next morning, nobody could find Harry.

2

When I walked into the upstairs hall the next morning, it was completely empty. No rug, no pictures, no table by the staircase. One bare light bulb stuck out from the wall like a sore nose. The movers must have started early.

I jumped down the stairs. All the furniture in the living room and dining room was gone.

We have to move a lot on account of my Dad's job. He's a computer software consultant. We usually don't stay in one place more than a year. I really can't stand all the relocating. But once we start packing up, I've got to admit, I just get excited. It's weird.

"Your brother awake, yet?" asked Mom.

"I guess so. He's not in his room," I answered.

"That's strange. We haven't seen him all morning," said Mom.

"It's not like Harry to disappear," Dad added, a worried look crossing his face like a cloud.

"I'll go find him," I volunteered. Suddenly, I thought that I had to know where Harry was. I don't really know why.

FRIGHT TIME

"First, breakfast," said Mom.

"Right," I said.

About five seconds later, I was out the door.

I headed straight for the mall. I thought maybe Harry zipped out early to get some fast food. "Anything but granola" will be Harry's dying words. But Harry wasn't there. He wasn't at the record store either.

I finally found him at a software store, of all places. I just walked up and watched without saying a word.

It was really strange. The sales guy had Harry's face up on the screen. Using a keyboard, he molded Harry's image as if it were clay.

First he pulled Harry's ears way out, then flapped them around, then tucked them back against his head.

Then he pulled Harry's jaw out and down so that he looked sort of apelike. He pushed back the top of Harry's forehead. He looked like some kind of other, unreal animal. It was really creepy. Somehow, the animal looked more like Harry than Harry himself.

I finally poked him.

"Mom and the Dad are looking for you," I said.

"Ugh," he grunted. He stood up and without

saying a word to me or to the sales guy, walked out of the store. And Harry didn't say a word to me all the way home. He just pulled a banana out of his jacket pocket, peeled it, tossed the peel right on the sidewalk, and walked along eating.

By the time we got home, Mom and Dad were already waiting in the car. We jumped in and hit the road. Six hours later we pulled into the driveway of our new home in Parksville.

It was a big old gray house, three stories high, with green shutters and a slate roof. A porch ran all across the front. And the front steps creaked when you stepped on them. Cool. I remember seeing a house just like it in an old scary TV show.

In the front yard was a tall oak tree and a really gnarled million-year-old beech. It had bumps and turns in its trunk that looked like bones or the twisted arms of giants.

Inside, the house was still empty. I don't believe in ghosts or anything like that. But this place felt, well, kind of *haunty*.

The place just felt like it belonged to someone else. I was glad when the moving van pulled up a little while later.

We all shifted into unpacking gear. Mom stood in the front hall like a traffic police officer and directed the moving guys. Dad, Harry, and I each took a third of the rooms, and began unpacking and putting away stuff.

We are really good at moving, mostly because we have had a lot of practice doing it. And it's always fun to do something that you're good at. This time, though, I was really glad to be so busy. It gave me less time to think about what was going on with Harry. He hadn't said a word during the whole ride here. He just grunted, looked out the window, and slept. Mom and Dad didn't even think it was weird.

I was even beginning to think that maybe it was all in my head.

Anyway, once we were in unpacking gear, Harry started looking and acting less weird.

Exhausted from all that unpacking, I tumbled into bed like a sack of wet laundry that night. But just as I was about to fall asleep, I thought I heard those same weird noises coming from Harry's room. But before I could move, I must have fallen asleep because the next thing I knew, I was dreaming.

I was in the middle of a dark jungle surrounded by strange-looking birds. They were huge, maybe six feet tall with dark wings and long red beaks. One of the birds walked up to me, snapped his beak open and shut, then walked away. His wing brushed against me as he turned. It wasn't covered with feathers. It was covered with fur.

Suddenly, all the birds started cackling at once and flapping their wings. Then the biggest of the flock bent over, coughing. I thought for a minute that he was going to throw up. But he heaved and heaved and coughed up a fur ball the size of my fist.

No. It wasn't a fur ball at all. It was a head. A shrunken head. I reached over to pick it up and it rolled away, opening its little mouth and laughing so loud the cackling birds fell silent.

I ran after it, but before I could reach it, I suddenly realized that I was awake and the sun was shining. And things really started to get hairy. I found out what the guy who used to live in my new house did, and I couldn't believe it.

3

I didn't have much time to think about my dream because we jumped right back into high

unpacking gear first thing in the morning. By
noon, we were finished. I was taking a well-de-
served rest in Dad's hammock, which is always
the first thing my dad puts up when we go to a
new place. I didn't know where Harry was.

I was just lying there, swinging slowly back
and forth when suddenly a silver flying saucer
flew over my head and landed a few feet away.

"Hi," said someone.

I twisted my head to see who was there.

"I'm Izzy. I guess we're neighbors," a blonde
girl said. "That's my frisbee."

"I'm Jesse," I said.

"So, you moved into the mad scientist's
house?" she said, tossing the frisbee up and
down.

"What?"

"The mad scientist, old man Albert. I live
right next door. I used to see him all the time.
He was really weird."

"How weird?" I asked. I was curious. Who
wouldn't be?

"He was always bringing animals into his
house during the day, but he never brought them
out until it was dark."

"That doesn't sound all that odd to me," I said,

kind of let down.

"Ahha!" she said, pointing a finger in the air. "But you don't know *why* he brought them out only at night."

I didn't say anything. She seemed okay, but there was a strange look in her eyes. I'm usually pretty cool around strangers. Right then, I wasn't sure what or who I was dealing with.

"He changed them," she whispered. "He took regular animals into his basement and he made them into freaks."

She had to be kidding, right? Somehow, I couldn't bring myself to say a word. But she must have seen something in my face.

"Don't believe me," she went on. "But I saw them, the freaks. He had a dog with two heads, and a cat with three tails."

She stood still for a second, her mouth open, her shoulders hunched. I could tell she was saving the best for last.

"And a sheep that mooed."

"Ah, that was some cheap trick," I answered, waving my hand.

"I don't know," said Izzy. "Maybe it was a trick. But there wasn't anything cheap about it. It looked real, right down to the burps and the way it smelled."

"And this guy made these animals somehow?"

She nodded. "Right here in your house, in his lab."

"There is no laboratory in my house," I said. I had been all through the house. I hadn't seen anything that looked like a laboratory.

"But there is," she said. "The day he moved out, the movers took out all kinds of lab equipment."

Dad can be pretty secretive when it comes to choosing a new house. But I was sure he would have told us if the previous occupant of the house had a lab.

"Anyway," she added, "you ought to look around. I'm sure you'll find a frog with six legs or something. Maybe then you'll believe me."

"Only if the frog bites me," I said.

She laughed and turned around and waved. It felt good to make a friend.

I rolled off the hammock and walked into the house as casually as I could. Then I went through every room of the house from the attic to the basement.

No lab. Nothing that even looked like a lab.

Something strange did happen, though.

SCARY HARRY

I was in the kitchen drinking some gorilla milk—that's what we call chocolate milk—when Harry walked in, carrying a grocery sack.

"Hey, Jess, want to shoot some hoops?" he asked, plopping the bag on the table. In the bag were about 10 pounds of bananas. I didn't think anything of it then. I was just glad to see Harry acting like his old self again.

"Sure, Harry," I said, even though I was beat from all the unpacking.

"Have some bananas," he said, handing me a whole bunch. "They're very good for you. I've already eaten five."

There was something about those bananas, let me tell you. Harry is older than I, and over an inch taller. But he hadn't beaten me in a game of one-on-one in about two years. Until that day. He beat me 11–2.

He played like a different guy. Like an animal. He wasn't hard or mean. He was completely unpredictable. Just when he looked like he was going to cut right, he went left. Just at the moment when he seemed ready to shoot, he would suddenly dribble around me and drive for the basket. He was impossible to stop. The game ended in about five minutes.

"I'm thinking of trying out for the team this year," said Harry, sitting down on the grass by the end of the driveway.

"No kidding? I thought you hated high school sports," I said.

He smiled, but said nothing. Then he pulled off his sneakers and socks and stretched his toes. I suddenly noticed how long his toes were.

"Want to see a trick?" he said.

Harry reached over with one foot and picked up a banana. Then he peeled it—with his feet! First he broke off the little stem and squeezed it between his big toe and the next one. Then he slowly pulled the skin down. He twisted the banana in his foot and did it again and again until the whole banana was peeled.

Okay, I would have been more impressed if he had done brain surgery with his feet, but I was pretty blown away anyhow.

"Too bad they don't have a team for fruit peeling," I joked.

He grinned, then shot the basketball right at my head. I ducked just in time.

"Hey, you jerk," I shouted.

Somehow, he pulled his lips back from his teeth and stuck out his lower jaw. It was really disgusting. And he laughed. It was like no other laugh I'd ever heard come from him. It was ugly. Mean. Like an animal.

I kept thinking that something really awful was happening to Harry. Very soon, I found out that I was right.

4

When I went to bed that night, I fell asleep quickly. Three seconds later, it seemed, I opened my eyes. My room was flooded with light.

It was the light beaming through my window from the big moon hanging over the beech tree in the backyard.

Just as I was about to roll over, I heard a noise. It was coming from Harry's room, and it was coming my way.

I slid out of my bed, stuck the pillow under the covers to make it look like I was sleeping, and crouched by the door.

Harry pushed my door open, and stepped into the room. I froze, my head pointed to the floor, and closed my eyes.

I could hear him breathing heavily through

his nose. The cuff of his pajama was just touching my wrist. If I moved even an inch, he'd catch me for sure. In the front hall all the way on the other side of the house, the grandfather clock beat out the time, tick-tock, tick-tock. Finally, he went into the hall. As soon as I heard him step on the squeaky stair at the top of the steps, I crept into the hall after him.

I stopped at the top of the stairs and peeked over the banister. Harry was heading for the basement, carrying a heavy bag. Something told me that the shrunken head was in that bag.

I waited for him to get ahead of me. I counted out 10 ticks of the clock, stepped over the squeaky stair, and tip-toed the rest of the way.

Harry had left the basement door open, but I couldn't see any light coming from down there. I stood still and listened with all my might.

Nothing. I waited. I closed my eyes to concentrate better. Nothing. Silence. Then...

BONG! BONG!

I jumped straight up in the air and caught my breath like I was drowning.

It was the clock striking.

Had Harry heard me? I listened again. Nothing. Then that tick-tock, tick-tock again.

I crept down the basement stairs. It was completely black. I had to feel my way along the wall in the dark, moving very slowly. There were still a lot of boxes in the basement, and I was afraid of banging into them.

I was about half way across the floor when it hit me. If I could barely move in this pitch blackness, how could Harry? And why couldn't I at least hear him? Where the heck did he go?

There were no windows in the basement, and only the one door that I had gone through. Harry had to be down here somewhere, but where? Was he waiting nearby to jump out at me? Was he trying to scare me? Did he know I followed him? Did I really want to know what he was doing in the middle of the night? What would he do if he caught me?

One by one, I felt the hairs rising on my neck. Funny chills ran up and down my arms and legs. I realized that someone was on the hall stairs. Was it Mom or Dad coming down to check out the noise?

No. The footsteps were going up the stairs!

That did it. I reached for the light switch and flipped it on.

There was no one in the basement but me.

FRIGHT TIME

And some boxes. Somehow, Harry had gotten around me. Or maybe he had never gone into the basement.

I walked toward the stairs. Then I stopped. Something was on the floor, an old newspaper. I picked it up. It was dated November 1, 1963. Why hadn't I noticed it before? I had been in and out of the basement a hundred times while we were unpacking.

It was a story about this 12-year old kid who one day just decided that he was going to live like a dog. He moved into a little house in his backyard, and slept out there. His parents fed him from a dog dish and put a dog collar on him and chained him up and everything. He stopped talking completely. He just barked.

They had pictures and everything, his dad holding the leash and his mom petting his head. They called him the Dog Boy. The story was probably fake, but I don't know. That picture looked real. Weird. I folded the paper and walked back upstairs.

Just as I closed the door to my room, a large hand fell on my shoulder like a slab of meat. The back of it was covered with bright red hair.

"Keep out of the basement, creep. And don't

try following me again, or I'll break your arm."

It was Harry. He had the nastiest look on his face that I have ever seen. His lips were drawn back from his teeth, as if he wanted to show me how sharp they were. And his eyes were dark and menacing.

I twisted away.

"I wasn't following you, Harry," I said. "I was looking for a bathroom. I thought there was one down there."

"Baloney," said Harry, moving his hand as if he were going to swat me.

But before he could hit me, I was in my room, grabbing the door.

I held the door closed and leaned against it, waiting for the sound of his footsteps going to his room. I could hear him breathing on the other side of the door. Finally, I heard him walk away.

All I could think about was that hand, and that thick red hair like a rusted steel wool pad. I couldn't get over how much Harry's hands looked like monkey hands. And Harry seemed so mean. Harry and I have had fights over the years. He always wins, which is no surprise because he's older, bigger, and stronger than I am. But I had never been afraid to take him on. At least, not until now.

One way or another, I was going to find out what was wrong with Harry.

The following day, Mom and Dad were out, which made my job a little bit easier, and a little bit scarier.

5

I woke up early the next morning to the smell of bacon cooking.

"Ah," I said to myself, "eggs and b." Bacon is one of those magic foods. You just can't eat too much of it. It's like ice cream or potato chips. Stuff you could just eat forever and never feel tired of.

We usually eat pretty healthy stuff in my house. And bacon, of course, isn't very good for you. If they were making bacon . . . I snapped my fingers. Suddenly it hit me.

"Uh-oh," I said to myself. That meant that Mom and Dad were making a getaway. Dad always likes to have what he calls "a big bad breakfast" before a long drive. Ever since Harry and I got old enough to take care of ourselves,

Mom and Dad have made a habit of going away for the weekend after we move into a new house.

I jumped out of bed, got dressed fast, pulled on my sneakers, pumped them up, and took the stairs four at a time.

I grabbed a cereal box and a bowl. I wanted to bring up how strange Harry had been acting, but I thought I would begin real casually. I thought about it, and thought about it, and thought about it. And then, "What's going on with Harry?" I practically shouted.

"What do you mean, son?" Dad asked.

"He's just acting so weird. Yesterday, he beat me at basketball. Then he threatened to beat me up. And he's eating tons of bananas like King Kong or something . . . "

"What's so weird about Harry beating you one-on-one? He's a lot older than you," Dad said.

"It's not just that . . . it's the bananas and everything," I said, starting to feel really dopey.

Mom smiled and glanced at Dad.

"Maybe Harry is just hungry," she said.

"But . . . "

"Hold it, Jesse," said Dad. "Let's take a little walk in the yard."

"I don't want to . . . " I started to say.

FRIGHT TIME

Dad stood up. I knew it was useless to resist. I got up and followed him into the backyard.

We walked along.

"Dad, I'm telling you the truth. Something is going on with Harry. I can't say exactly what it is, but it's something strange." I kicked a dandelion's head off.

"You know, Jesse," said Dad, picking up a stick, "I have noticed that you guys haven't been hanging around with each other as usual. Usually when we move into one of these towns, you two are like Batman and Robin."

"It's because he's being so odd, Dad. He disappears without telling me where he's going or when he's coming back. He doesn't want me around," I added, suddenly realizing how much that bothered me.

"You know, there are times during their lives when brothers just don't get along, Jesse. Sometimes your Uncle Barnaby and I don't get along, and sometimes you and Harry don't. It's not that one is right and the other is wrong. It's just that sometimes brothers get into different things at different times.

"And I think that this is one of those times with Harry," he said. "He's 14. That's a tough age. He's changing in lots of ways!"

"I don't know, Dad. I guess it's just that . . . well, he's being such a creep about everything."

"Listen, cowboy," he said. "This trouble between you and Harry . . . I want you guys to work it out between yourselves."

"But, Dad . . ."

"No buts, Jesse. Your mother and I are going away for the weekend. We've been planning this trip since we knew we had to move. I don't want to have to worry about you guys, and I don't want your mother worrying either. So find a way to work it out. I mean it."

I opened my mouth to say something. Then I closed it.

We turned around and headed back to the kitchen. Harry was sitting at the table in a dark blue turtleneck shirt. I thought that was pretty weird, because it was already pretty hot, and was supposed to get hotter. He reached to pour some milk in his cereal, and I had to blink. His arm stuck out of the end of his sleeve by about three inches.

"Oh dear, Harry," said Mom. "That shirt is too small for you. So much for buying pre-shrunk clothing."

FRIGHT TIME

How could they miss it? Harry's shirt hadn't shrunk! His arms were getting longer and longer, and hairier and hairier. Why was I the only one who could see it? Didn't they realize what was happening? How could they be so blind?

Mom and Dad left for their trip later that morning. I have to admit, I was sort of glad to see them go. I wanted to get started gathering the evidence. I was playing it as cool as I could. But it wasn't easy. I mean, not only couldn't they see what was happening, they thought *I* was being a jerk!

Harry and I waved good-bye to them as they pulled out of the driveway. Harry had his arm around my shoulders, being chummy as in the old days. But as soon as the car drove around the curve and out of sight, he pulled a banana out of his pocket and walked away from me without a word.

I turned around and headed for Izzy's house.

"Glad to see you, Jesse," said Izzy, waving me into the kitchen. "Got something to show you."

I walked into the kitchen. She was wearing pink sweatpants and a tee shirt. She had her hair pulled back into three ponytails. I liked Izzy. I felt like we were friends already.

She unrolled a big piece of blue paper.

"My mom works for the real estate agency that rented you your house. So I stopped by there yesterday and borrowed the plans."

"Which one is the basement?" I asked.

"Basement?"

"Yeah. I figure that the lab had to be in the basement."

"So, you believe me about old man Albert, the mad scientist."

"More than that," I said. "I think that maybe something is happening to my brother. In fact, I'm sure of it. I just have to get some proof."

"For who, the police?"

"No! No way would I ever do anything that could get my brother in trouble. I tried to tell my mom and dad, but they think I'm just being a creep. You know, sibling rivalry, all that sort of stuff. I've got to get some proof of what's going on. I'm really worried about Harry."

She nodded her head and got real serious.

We looked at the plans.

"You see," she said, "each little box is a room. This is the living room. This is the dining room, kitchen, and so on."

I quickly counted all the boxes and then tried

to imagine all the rooms in the house.

"There's no room that could a lab. There's a room for each one of these boxes," I said, suddenly disappointed.

We stared at the blueprint of the basement for a while. Along the margins were numbers telling you how long each wall was, and little pictures for where the boiler goes and stuff like that.

Then I noticed something. "What's this?" I asked, pointing to a little break in the line that was supposed to be the wall.

"I don't know."

That's when I got my big idea, which led to an even bigger discovery.

6

My idea was simple. The lab had to be somewhere in the house. Since we had the plans for the whole house, and the plans had all the measurements for all the rooms, all we had to do was account for all the space listed on the blueprint. If the house had fewer square feet than the plans said it did, then we would know that there was a secret room somewhere. All we had to do was measure every room and compare the result to what the plan said.

We started in the living room.

Izzy stood at one end of the room and held the measuring tape against the wall. I walked to the other end of the room, pulling the tape with me. It was a big room, 10 feet by 20 feet, according to the plan. I walked across the room and counted, "Ten, nine, eight, seven, six, five, four, three, two, one."

"Ten feet exactly," said Izzy, disappointed.

We measured the other way, and it came out 20 feet exactly.

I had to admit, I was down. There's something about having a good idea that makes it really hard when it doesn't produce a good result.

We moved onto the dining room, and had no better luck. It measured perfectly, too.

"Let's forget it," I said as I rewound the tape. "It was a stupid idea, anyway."

"No, it wasn't," said Izzy. "Come on, let's try the basement. Who ever heard of a secret lab hidden in a dining room, anyway?"

She had a point.

We went down the stairs into the dark basement and started measuring.

FRIGHT TIME

First we measured the width. Izzy held the tape against the wall. I walked slowly across the room. "Twenty-five feet," I said.

"That checks," said Izzy. "According to the plan, the basement measures 25 by 40."

Next, we checked the length. Izzy stood at the far end, and I walked toward the other end, trying to walk as straight as I could. When I got to the wall, I stopped and looked at the tape. It reached 30. I couldn't believe my eyes!

"Thirty feet, Izzy."

"What?" she called from the other end of the basement. "You sure?"

I looked at the tape again. "I'm sure."

"Ya-hoo!" she shouted. "We found it!"

She ran to my end of the basement and walked along the wall.

"What are you doing?" I asked.

"Looking for a secret door, I guess."

We walked up and down the wall looking for any sign of a door. But we couldn't find a thing. Everywhere we tapped, it sounded solid. There didn't seem to be anything like a door.

"You sure of the measurements?" I asked.

"Yeah."

We looked at the plans again.

"What's this?" I asked, pointing to a break in a line on the plans.

Izzy shook her head, then she looked at the plans for the other floors of the house.

"I think it's a window," she said at last.

"But there's no window in this wall," I said.

I pointed to a larger break in the line.

"And this," I said. "This looks like a door. The lab has got to be behind this wall!"

Izzy shook her head slowly.

Then it hit me again, another idea.

"Come on, Izzy," I almost shouted, moving toward the stairs. "Let's check outside."

The basement wall we were looking at was in the back of the house. Shrubs and flowers were planted all along it, so you couldn't see it clearly.

I poked around in the azalea bushes.

"Look!" I shouted. "A window!"

It was half below the ground. The glass had been painted black. And it was closed and locked, which didn't matter all that much because I didn't think I could fit through it anyway.

"Put it there, Sherlock!" shouted Izzy, giving me five. "Now let's find that door!"

We studied the plans again. The door should be about eight feet to the right of the window.

FRIGHT TIME

But there was no door in sight.

"It's got to be here somewhere," said Izzy. "It isn't very easy to hide a door."

I pushed my way back to the window, got on my hands and knees, and crawled along the side of the house, going over every inch of the wall. Nothing. Nothing but mud and scratches from the bushes. I stood up and started to walk away from the house. But as I stepped through the dirt, I caught my foot on a root, tripped, and fell with a thud, a very strange-sounding thud.

I jumped to my feet. We began digging furiously in the dirt with our hands. About three inches down, we found it—a steel cellar door set in the ground.

"Looks like someone went through a lot of trouble to hide this door," I said.

"Like your brother?" Izzy asked quietly.

I nodded my head and pulled at the heavy padlock on the door. It was brand new. It still had the price tag on it.

"This lock hasn't been buried very long, that's for sure," I said.

"This is really getting scary," Izzy whispered.

"We've got to get in there," I said. "There's got to be something in there to prove to them that something really is wrong with Harry."

"Jesse," whispered Izzy. "Suppose it's one of those creatures from that guy I was telling you about. Suppose he left it behind?"

I stopped and looked at her hard.

"You mean that's true?" I asked.

She nodded her head. She was scared. I hadn't really believed what she had told me . . . until now. And I have to admit, I didn't like believing her at all.

"No way can it be some kind of animal," I said, trying to sound confident. "Someone would have heard it."

"I don't know about that," said Izzy. "Lots of animals that are dangerous don't make noise. I read on the back of a juice box that cheetahs can't roar or anything. And snakes, Jesse, snakes don't make a lot of noise."

"I hate snakes," I said.

Suddenly, we heard the front door open and close.

"Harry is back," I shout-whispered.

We quickly kicked the dirt back over the door. It was a good thing we hadn't uncovered the whole door. We finished quickly.

By the time Harry strolled into the backyard,

Fright Time

Izzy and I were tossing frisbees.

I knew that I had to get into the basement, but how? Harry must have the key. How could I get it from him? And what would he do if he caught me?

7

I couldn't believe myself a couple of hours later. After supper I lounged around watching TV. I was waiting for Harry to take his shower. My plan was to "borrow" his keys while he was in the shower, race downstairs, open the lock, run back upstairs, and return his keys . . . all before he finished his shower.

As soon as I heard the water running in the upstairs bathroom, I made my move.

I started up the stairs one by one. The bathroom was at the far end of the hall right next to Harry's room. That meant that I would have to get all the way down the hall from the landing into his room without his hearing me.

I reached the top of the steps and looked down the hall. It suddenly seemed very, very long. I could barely hear the noise of the shower, but every sound that I made seemed to bounce off the walls and be magnified in my ears.

I started to walk slowly down the hall, trying to be as quiet as I could, but of course, the first step I took was on the creaky stair! I froze for a second. Then I started to think, if I'm too slow, Harry will finish his shower before I can get the keys. I unfroze, and hurried down the hall.

And almost tripped over the telephone cord for the hall phone on the table outside Harry's room!

I got to his room and slipped inside. I looked around and . . . great . . . his keys were on his bed, and there, shiny-new on the ring, was a key for a padlock!

First, I memorized exactly where the keys were on the bed. Then I picked them up carefully, slipped out of his room, and tip-toed down the hall and down the stairs.

Once I was on the first floor, I raced through the house, and out the back and into the yard.

I looked up at the side of the house. I could still hear the shower running.

Good. I felt in the dirt, found the lock, and tried the key.

It fit perfectly! I turned it. Click!

I was tempted to just take a peek in the secret room right then, but I resisted, just barely. Jumping up, I ran into the house, making sure that the shower was still on. I have to admit, though, I had no idea what I would do or say if Harry caught me.

Then I started up the stairs. Just when I got to the landing . . . the hall phone rang!

I froze.

I couldn't stop to answer it. Harry might come out of the bathroom before I got the keys back, and there was no telling what would happen then!

I was tempted to make a run for it, but I suddenly realized that I really had to be quiet. If Harry heard me in the hall, he would wonder why I wasn't answering the phone.

I had to get those keys back!

I started to tip-toe as quickly as I could down the hall.

"Jesse! Answer the phone!" shouted Harry. No way, I thought.

I made it to his door and turned the knob.

"Jesse, you jerk! Answer that phone!"

I pushed open the door. Suddenly the water in the shower stopped!

I hurried over to the bed and placed the keys exactly the way they were before.

"Jesse! You little creep!"

I started for his door. The bathroom door opened. I froze. If he caught me in his room, I was dead.

I heard him pick up the phone. I dove under his bed. I just barely fit. There was a cardboard box under there. A funny smell was coming from it. I peeked into it. Bananas! Harry had an entire box of bananas under his bed.

Harry picked up the phone. "Yeah, who is this?" he asked. He was angry.

"Who?" said Harry. "Izzy? Izzy who?" Then in a loud voice he called, "Jesse! Phone!"

Izzy! What a time for her to call!

"Jesse, you jerk! Phone!" Harry called.

I heard him put the phone down on the table without hanging up.

Then I heard the door to his room open. I caught my breath.

From where I was lying under the bed, I could see his feet. Now they were covered with thick black hair. The toes seemed about twice as long as they used to be, almost like fingers. And they were walking toward the bed.

Suddenly they turned around, as Harry sat down on the bed. I felt the mattress push against my back. A second later he stood up.

His feet moved away from the bed. Then his hands appeared on the floor, right next to his feet. Then his feet went up into the air! I could only see his hands, those hairy hands.

I heard Harry grunt, and the hands started to move around the room.

Harry was walking on his hands!

It got even stranger. The hands walked over to Harry's stereo and suddenly, music came on! He must have turned on the stereo with his feet.

I was very tempted to peek just once to see just what he was doing and how he was doing it. If I was real careful, maybe he wouldn't see me. And even if he did, hey, he was still my brother. We were still best friends.

Just then, Harry cursed real loud, using a word I had never heard him use before. A really bad one. A bunch of CDs fell to the floor. One spilled out of its case and was rolling right toward me.

Then the hands started to walk toward me. Now, I was really dead meat, I thought.

The hands stopped right in front of the bed. I

held my breath and pushed the CD toward Harry.

Suddenly, his foot appeared and edged its way under the bed. I slid the CD toward him. His long toes—this close up, they seemed to move like snakes—spread, flexed, and grasped the disc. He turned it sideways and pulled it out from under the bed.

I finally breathed out, very slowly. That was a close call. But even while Harry was flexing his toes, I couldn't help notice that his feet smelled funky, even though he just finished showering. Not funky like sneakers, funky like the ape house at the zoo. And crawling around in the hair on the back of his feet were fleas!

If Mom and Dad came home right now, all I would have to do is show them Harry's feet, and they would know that something was wrong. Harry's feet were no longer human. What did that mean about Harry?

I looked out again. Harry walked over to his basketball. His feet reached down to pick it up. But he dropped it. Then he dropped it again.

Harry cursed again and flipped back to his feet. He must have grabbed the basketball and thrown it through the window because the next noise I heard was shattering glass!

Then he really started cursing, really bad curses. But instead of just saying the curse, he was spitting it. From the noise he was making, I guessed he was pounding his chest Tarzan-style, and he was definitely grunting and hissing.

Then he suddenly flopped down on his bed.

"Food!" I think he said.

His hand appeared by the side of the bed. He was reaching under for the bananas. But he couldn't reach it, even though his arms were very long.

I saw his feet on the floor, then his lower leg and knee, both of which were even hairier than his toes. This was it. He was going to kneel down on the floor, look under the bed, and see me. I was doomed.

A hand appeared on the floor.

And then the doorbell rang.

Harry cursed and stood up.

The doorbell rang again and again.

I heard the sounds of Harry getting dressed, then walking out of his room and going down the stairs.

I slipped out from under the bed and darted into the hall. Izzy had come to the door! I tip-toed down the hall, hanging up the phone because it was making that funny noise phones make when they're off the hook.

I'm not sure Izzy knew my predicament, but she kept Harry occupied at the front door while I slipped down the stairs into the family room. I lay down on the couch and pretended to be asleep for a second. Then I jumped up and walked into the front hall as innocent as could be.

Izzy was still talking to Harry, although to be accurate, Harry wasn't saying very much.

"So, when I didn't get an answer on the phone, I began to wonder what was going on," Izzy was saying. "Then I heard the window break, and I thought there might be trouble."

"Nothing wrong around here, Izzy," I said.

Harry turned around, took one look at me, then without a word, walked back up the stairs.

Izzy and I just looked at each other for a second.

"It was this close," I whispered. "Why did you call?"

"I wanted to see if you got the key."

"I did. Izzy, I'm really scared for Harry."

Suddenly Izzy held up her hand.

"He's coming back," she hissed at me.

Harry walked up behind me.

"Hey, squirt," said Harry. "Tell your friend to beat it."

"See you later," Izzy said, trying to let Harry's nasty tone of voice roll off her back.

She winked at me and walked away. According to our plan, I was going to call her when it was time to sneak into the secret lab.

I had hoped to make my move that night. But that idea vanished quickly. Instead of heading for his bedroom, as I expected him to, Harry went into the basement.

I climbed the stairs to my room. When I got to the top, I stopped like a deer caught in the headlights of a car.

The hall phone! I had hung it up! Had Harry noticed it when he went upstairs?

If he did, then he knew I wasn't in the family room when Izzy rang the bell. And if he knew that, I was really in trouble.

I may have hung up the phone without thinking, but when I went to bed that night, I made up for lost time by thinking for hours about what had happened.

This was much worse than the story of that kid who decided to become a dog. That kid didn't look any different. He was still a kid. And at least dogs were friendly. My brother wasn't just acting like a gorilla, he was turning into one, a really nasty one.

I remember visiting the zoo once and going to the ape house. There was this one gorilla named Cody. He was sitting in his cage, just staring up at the ceiling and holding a doll in his hands.

I stared at that gorilla for a long time. But just as I was about to leave, he suddenly turned toward me and looked right into my eyes.

Then he ripped the doll's head off and threw it at me. Two days later, I read in the paper that that ape had killed one of the other apes.

That night, I lay in bed with my samurai sword lying on the floor right where I could reach it. I didn't even try to go to sleep. But I could remember hearing the big hall clock strike midnight, and the very next thing I knew, it was morning.

I got dressed right away and was just finishing my cereal when I heard Harry shuffling down the stairs. He walked into the kitchen, carrying a bunch of bananas. He looked more like an ape than ever.

He was unbelievably hairy. His face was covered with stubble, which would have looked cool except that his neck was even hairier than his face.

He was wearing shorts, and his legs were very hairy, too. In fact it was almost as if he had fur instead of hair.

"Morning, Harry," I said.

He looked in my direction for a second, grunted, peeled a banana, and ate it in about three seconds.

Then he stood at the kitchen sink, turned on the water, and hunched over the faucet. He scooped up handfuls of water and ate another seven bananas in silence. Every once in a while, he would pick a flea from his neck or from the matted hair on his legs.

He just stood there and ate banana after banana, scooping up water with his hands. When he was finished, he walked out of the kitchen into the backyard.

A few minutes later, I saw him walk around the side of the house carrying his favorite basketball. He was grunting and dribbling.

"That's right," I said to no one in particular. "Today's the basketball tryouts!"

Parkville High was holding tryouts for freshmen this weekend. And Harry had said he was thinking of trying out for the team. That must be where he was going.

It made me feel sad. Ordinarily, Harry and I would have talked for hours about something as important as trying out for a sport. But this time, he had said nothing about it at all.

On the other hand, it meant that Harry wouldn't be around for a while. So I dialed Izzy's number.

"Hello," said the voice on the other end of the line.

"Ah...it's Jesse. I, I live next door." Then I asked for Izzy.

"Hi, Jesse."

"Harry's gone at least for a couple of hours," I said. "Do you feel like doing some..."

"I'm on my way over," she said before I finished talking.

I put down the phone and took a deep breath. It was time. Very soon, I would know a lot more about what was wrong with Harry.

FRIGHT TIME

Just then, someone knocked at the door. I jumped. It was Izzy.

I stepped outside. She had a flashlight and was wearing a baseball cap.

"Let's go, Sherlock," she said.

"Okay," I replied.

We walked to the back of the house. The first thing we saw stopped us in our tracks.

It was a squirrel, a very dead squirrel. It was lying right in the spot where the door was buried. Its head was twisted to one side and its fur was matted with what looked like dried blood. But worst of all were its legs. They were frozen in a running position as if it had died still trying to run away.

Izzy and I looked at each other. She never said a word, but I was sure that she was thinking the same thing I was. She was thinking that Harry killed that squirrel and left it on the door as a warning. I was thinking the same thing. But at the same time, I didn't believe it.

"It was probably a dog," I said. "A dog killed it."

"Yeah," said Izzy. "You can tell from the uh . . . blood. Some animal obviously bit this squirrel."

"Yeah. That's obvious."

I found a shovel and moved the squirrel to one side.

"Don't bury it," said Izzy. "We'll want to put it back just where it was, right? I mean just in case Harry . . . "

"Yeah," I said, quickly. I didn't want her to finish saying what she was going to say.

We scraped the dirt off the door, and for the second time stopped in our tracks.

The lock was locked again.

"Well," said Izzy, "That answers one question. He knows that we know."

We both looked over at the squirrel. I don't know about Izzy, but I wanted to run. Then from somewhere deep inside me, a voice said, "Okay. Let's break in. We have nothing to lose."

Izzy looked over at me. Then like a caterpillar changing direction, her lips turned up slowly into a smile.

I got a crowbar from Dad's tool box, and got to work. I slid the crowbar under the hasp, and pulled with all my strength. I pulled so hard, I thought my nose would bleed. Just when I thought I couldn't pull any harder, the lock popped off!

"Wow," said Izzy.

I looked at her. Then I pulled the door up and open. It creaked just like old doors in horror movies.

The light streamed down onto concrete stairs. I put my foot on the first step.

"Do you think that there's anything, you know, alive down there?" Izzy asked.

"I don't know, Izzy," I replied. "But we're going to find out. Come on."

I continued down. Izzy followed close behind. There were only seven steps. But it was the longest flight of stairs I ever walked down.

The air was damp. Mold grew on the floor. I could smell water somewhere, and bananas.

I shone the light around the long narrow room, expecting to see, I don't know what, monsters or something. Instead, I saw flower pots, potting soil, stuff like that.

The walls had been painted a sick-looking green recently. So had the ceiling, which was a little weird. But that was it. Nothing mysterious at all. All this worry, only to find an empty room.

"Take a look at this," Izzy called from a corner of the room.

It was a locker like the ones we have in school.

Izzy pulled out a windbreaker.

"I'll bet that your brother wears a medium jacket," said Izzy.

I looked at it. It was Harry's, all right. Suddenly, Izzy screamed.

Something crashed to the floor. An awful smell flooded the room. Some kind of fluid washed over my sneakers. I looked down. Lying about two inches from my left sneaker were three human ears!

I almost screamed, too. "Oh, gross!"

"They were in a jar in the locker," said Izzy.

"In a jar. Ears in a jar! That's got to be the most disgusting thing I have ever seen!"

She started to move toward the door.

"I'm sorry, Jesse. But I've just got to get out of here. This place is giving me the creeps."

"Okay, Izzy," I said. "Let's go."

We turned to go. But suddenly the door slammed shut!

Izzy screamed. And I think that I did, too. I was so surprised that I dropped the flashlight, which immediately fell apart, throwing us into total darkness. When I caught my breath, I heard footsteps coming our way.

9

Izzy grabbed my arm and squeezed it so tight it hurt. We didn't say a word. We just listened. The footsteps moved closer. We could hear heavy breathing now, too. We didn't dare move. Finally, whatever it was stopped walking and sighed.

"So you brought her down here, too." It was Harry.

"Harry!" I almost shouted. "You scared the daylights out of us. Do you have a flashlight? Mine broke when I dropped it."

"You had to come down here, didn't you?" Harry sounded like he was thinking of doing something really bad.

"Hey, kids are supposed to be curious," said Izzy. She was trying to sound casual. But it wasn't working.

"Curiosity killed the cat," hissed Harry.

Or squirrel, I thought to myself.

"Ha, ha," said Izzy, trying to pass off Harry's comment as a lighthearted joke.

Suddenly Harry's hand (I was tempted to call

it a paw) touched my shoulder. "I'll get to you in a minute, creepy. But as for you . . ."

He took Izzy's arm. She must have been really scared. I was.

"You," Harry continued to Izzy, "will have to go, right now."

He led Izzy away into the darkest corner of the room. They whispered for a few seconds. Then I heard a long, low creak.

"She's gone," said Harry from the far end of the room. "She won't be bothering us now."

I gulped.

Harry's footsteps moved closer to me, then stopped. "I sent her home. She won't say anything to anyone, will she?"

"No way. Not if she promised not to," I said, breathing for the first time in about five minutes. "She's a good kid."

Harry chuckled. "No, she won't talk to anyone. She knows what it would mean for you."

Suddenly he stopped laughing. He flicked a switch and his face was illuminated by flashlight. His jaw stuck way out, and he was hairier than ever. His eyebrows went straight across his forehead.

"Here I am, Jesse. You found me out."

"Harry, what's going on?"

"What's the matter, Jesse? Scared?"

I was very scared. But no way was I going to let him know it.

"No," I said. "You're my brother, Harry. I'm not scared of you."

He grinned again and laughed, slapping his hand on his thigh with a very loud smack.

"Harry, what's going on with you? What's wrong with you?"

"Wrong? Nothing is wrong, Jesse boy. Absolutely nothing. It's just that I'm changing, don't you see?"

"Yes, I see that," I said.

"You want to know the whole story?"

I nodded.

"Okay, but first you've got to swear to tell no one. And that includes your little friend."

"Okay," I said.

"No. Words aren't enough. This is a promise we have to seal in blood."

"Okay," I said. As we had done a hundred times before, we each pricked our fingers with a pin, squeezed some blood out, and rubbed our fingers together. I can't tell you why we did it all those times in the past because I still have to keep those secrets.

He switched on a light. The secret room suddenly didn't look so scary. But there was something that I hadn't noticed before. It looked like a trap door.

He walked me over to it. It was a thin wooden grating over what looked like a sewer or something.

"When I found this room, I didn't think much of it. I figured that the old guy who lived here never used it. Anyway, I was just walking around when I fell through this grating."

He kicked a bottle cap into the grating. It splashed at the bottom.

"It's filled with some kind of fluid, sweet-smelling stuff. Anyway, I fell through the grate and landed in it, and it took 20 minutes to get out. But it was weird. I wasn't in any hurry. I wasn't scared or anything. I kind of liked the way it felt. When I finally did get out, I felt different. Look!"

He held out his arm. It was even longer than the day before, very muscular, and very, very hairy. He flexed his biceps. The muscle bulged.

"Tonight I'll take one long soak, and then, I

think, I'll be done," he said, his eyes shining.

He threw his very long, very hairy arm around my shoulders.

"Then, creepy, it's your turn."

10

It took all the will power I had not to pull away and run. But I had to ask one question.

"Harry, what about the shrunken head? The one Uncle Barnaby gave you?"

His face went blank for a second. Then he smiled, I think.

"Shrunken head! That was no shrunken head. Uncle Barnaby gave me an electric razor!"

So that was the sound I had heard, an electric razor!

"But," Harry went on, "I didn't have to shave. So, I was pretty peeved that he gave it to me. And now look at me! Suddenly, I'm as hairy as an ape! And I feel powerful. Really powerful. And I am."

He turned in a slow circle, his arms above his head. He *was* as hairy as an ape. His whole body was turning into an ape's body. It was disgusting. And it was going to get worse.

I was a little surprised when Harry let me go. At first I thought it was a trick. But I finally took it as a good sign. It meant that he still trusted that I would abide by our blood oath. Or that he didn't care.

Part of me just wanted to call Mom and Dad. But I figured that by the time they got back, it would be too late. And the police would never believe me. Harry wasn't an ape yet, and no one in this town knew what my brother was like except me.

On the other hand, Harry had promised to throw me in that pool. I didn't want to turn into an ape. I couldn't help but think about that squirrel and the way its head was twisted.

I called Izzy as soon as Harry let me out of the cellar and told her to find out from her mother where old man Albert had moved.

The next morning we were up at 6:00 a.m. and on a bus to Killian, the next town.

The house was on a quiet, tree-lined street. It hardly seemed like the kind of place to be home to a mad scientist.

Still, you never know. The scariest people can sometimes turn up in the safest-looking place.

FRIGHT TIME

When we knocked on the door, Izzy and I were ready for Mr. Albert to come to the door with a chain saw or an ax.

The man who answered the door looked like an egg. He was short, round, and completely bald. I mean, there wasn't a hair on his head.

"May I help you?" he asked.

"Help us!" I practically shouted. "Are you the man who used to live at 485 Monroe Avenue in Parkville?"

He nodded his head slowly. His smile was gone.

"Well, my brother fell into some chemicals you left in the basement, and now . . ."

"Oh, dear!" said Mr. Albert, catching his face in his hands. "I thought I sealed that vat securely."

He waved us into his house. As I looked around, I almost passed out. All around the room were shelves and shelves of jars and jars of pickled animal parts: bat ears, sloth toes, eyes of all kinds. You name it, he had a jar of it.

"Sit down, please," he said. We did.

"I am sorry that something happened to your brother," he said. "I'm sure that I can fix it, as soon as I know a little more about the incident."

I ran through the story quickly. The whole time, he kept his head down and stared at the floor. From time to time, he would go "Tsk, tsk, tsk."

When I finished he looked up at me. I thought he was going to cry.

"I never wanted to hurt anyone," he said. "You see, I am a veterinary surgeon. I work with Gerry's Giant Three Ring Circus. I take care of the animals. I also used to help make animals. You may have heard about Gerry's Giant Unicorn?"

I nodded yes. I had seen it about three years before.

"I created that by grafting a goat's horn onto a Shetland pony's head."

I didn't tell him that I had believed it was real.

"But I became concerned that maybe I was hurting these animals. I wanted to find a better way. So, I began to experiment with biochemical techniques that allowed me to take traits from one species and get them to grow naturally in another. I had some early successes with dogs, cats, and a sheep.

"Then I transferred traits by mixing the creatures' bloods. Later I developed the soaking technique. And I was working on an experiment with orangutans. But one by one my creatures began to go mad and they had to be destroyed.

"I realized that I was doing something very wrong. So I stopped. I quit the circus, sold my house, and now I am going to retire. In fact, I am leaving town for good tomorrow, and going south."

"Mr. Albert, wait a minute," I said. "Do you mean that my brother Harry is turning into an orangutan and that he could be going insane?"

"Oh, no, no, that won't happen. Not if you stop it before the new process has time to alter his basic metabolic functions."

"What?" I said. I didn't know what he was talking about.

He went to a closet and took out what looked like a fire extinguisher.

"Spray him with this. Thoroughly. It will reverse the process. Then empty what is left into the vat to neutralize the solution. After that you can dump the solution wherever you want. It will be changed into salt water. But you must do it quickly before it's too late."

We grabbed the antidote and ran.

11

The bus ride home was only about 45 minutes long, but it felt like hours. I was having trouble carrying the antidote.

When we walked into the house, it was completely quiet. No radio. No TV. Nothing. I never knew how scary a quiet house could feel until then. If there's noise, at least you know where the trouble is. Quiet means that trouble could be around any corner and come at any time.

We started up the stairs to Harry's room. Then it hit me. The big clock in the front hall, why didn't I hear it? I craned my neck over the banister. The glass over the face of the clock was smashed and scattered all over the place. The hands of the clock were twisted, and the big brass pendulum was lying on the floor. The steel bar that held the weight was about a half-inch thick. It was bent.

I stood totally still and held my breath. It must have sounded like doomsday when Harry wrecked the clock. Why had he done it? Had I come too late? Was he waiting for me upstairs? Downstairs? Around the next corner? Part of me wanted to run as far away as I could. A big part of me.

Izzy poked me in the back. I put my foot on the next step up and kept going. It isn't easy being a brother.

We got to the top of the stairs. I stepped over the creaky step and flattened myself against the wall. Izzy started to follow. I gestured to her to step over the noisy stair, but she looked at me without understanding, until she heard the stair creak.

I held my breath. Izzy jumped to my side. And, I hate to admit this, I closed my eyes.

The door to Harry's room stayed closed.

I breathed very quietly. Then, it began to open very, very slowly.

Izzy nodded down the stairs. We had left the front door open. It was the wind. I turned back to Harry's room. I couldn't believe my eyes.

Not Harry, but an orangutan wearing Harry's gym shorts, was sitting on a chair, his back toward us. He was completely covered with reddish-brown hair. His long arms hung to the floor, and his knuckles rested on the rug. And he smelled like the ape house at the zoo.

A pile of banana peels lay on the side. He was

looking out the window, which looked out over the front walk.

"Uh-oh," I said to myself. If Harry was looking out his window, then he knew we were in the house. At that exact second, he turned around.

He looked right at me. His eyes were sad. He climbed off the chair and moved toward me. I heard Izzy gulp.

"Get the antidote ready," she whispered.

Harry lumbered closer, never taking his eyes off me, still staring at me with that sad look. He reached the door to his room, and slowly closed it.

Izzy and I looked at each other. This was going to be easier than either of us thought. We walked right up and opened his door. He was back in his chair, staring out the window. But he spun around in a flash and let out a screech that I swear made every hair on the back of my neck stand up.

He grabbed a baseball bat and charged at me. Izzy backed out quickly, but so did I. When I tried to backpedal, I tripped over her and fell backward. That was lucky because just as I fell back, Harry swung the bat, missed me completely, and fell on top of us.

I pushed him off and back into his room. Izzy

jumped up and raced for the stairs.

"I'm calling the police. He's dangerous!" she shouted.

The tank of antidote began barreling down the stairs. Suddenly the house was anything but quiet.

"Don't call the police, Izzy," I shouted. "We've got to give him the antidote."

I pulled Harry's door closed and held it.

Izzy hadn't heard me. I could hear her dialing the phone in the kitchen downstairs. If the police got here before I treated Harry, they would just take him away. By the time I explained everything, it would be too late. My brother would be an orangutan forever.

Suddenly the doorknob went loose. I heard Harry throwing open the window of his room. He'll be climbing out and coming around through the front door, which we had left open.

The samurai sword! I ran into my room. I pulled it out of the scabbard and ran into the hall. I was just hoping that Harry would be human enough to be frightened by the look of it. I knew I could never really try to hurt him with it.

Suddenly he appeared at the front door, swinging the bat just as Izzy ran into the front hall. It was now or never.

I howled like a wild dog and charged down the stairs, waving the sword over my head, just like in the movies. Harry froze in his tracks, then backed out the front door.

He ran around the back and I followed.

"Wait here, Izzy," I shouted as I raced out.

Once in the backyard, Harry threw open the cellar door and dropped into the darkness. Now it was my turn to freeze. He knew the inside of that cellar like the inside of his own room. In the dark, he would have a big advantage. And the vat was down there. Hadn't he promised to give me the treatment?

"Jesse, come down here!"

It was Harry. He could still talk! That meant it was not too late. I could still save him.

Suddenly police sirens sounded in the distance. They were coming this way.

I peered into the darkness of the secret room.

"Jesse, come on down here. I won't hurt you. Come on, we're brothers."

I backed up a few steps and then took a flying leap down the seven stairs into the basement. As I landed, I dropped to my knees and rolled to the wall.

FRIGHT TIME

And just in time, too. Harry had swung the bat right at where my head would have been.

I spun around and held up the sword vertically, my back to the wall. From this angle, Harry would have to pass into the light coming through the cellar door to get at me.

A second later he did, swinging the bat low and hard. I flipped the sword down, blocking the blow, but it threw me off balance. I fell, and rolled again into the darkness. My sword skittered across the floor and fell into the vat with a splash.

Harry stood up in the sunlight, the bat in his hand. "Don't you see, Jesse? It's only a matter of time before you take your little bath. I am bigger, and much, much stronger than you. You will never be able to stop me. All it takes is a bath . . . and in a few days, we'll be brothers again."

I stood up and walked toward Harry. As soon as he lowered that bat, I was going to jump him.

"Okay, Harry," I said. "Truce."

He stood back for a second, then he smiled. "I'm glad, you . . . "

Suddenly his face got all twisted up, as if he couldn't get the words out.

"Jesse . . . Jesse agggahhghnn."

His eyes got this panicked look in them. He started to jabber, making monkey noises as he got more and more angry.

"Harry," I shouted, "Try to keep calm . . . I can help you . . ."

He jumped away from me, jabbering faster and faster. Then he became enraged and began swinging the bat all over the place.

I heared the police cars turning onto our block.

Suddenly, Izzy appeared at the cellar stairs. She had the antidote in her hands.

My only chance was to maneuver Harry into position for Izzy to soak him with the cure.

It wasn't going to be easy. Harry was going bananas with that baseball bat. He was smashing flower pots and banging the walls.

The police cars were pulling up in front of the house.

"Jesse!" shouted Izzy. "There's no more time!"

She was right. I just put my head down and ran at Harry screaming as loud as I could. I grabbed the bat with one hand, and swung him around toward the stairs. He tripped and fell backward.

"Yes!" cried Izzy, spraying him completely

with the antidote, covering him from head to foot.

Harry started to get up, but then fell back, and crawled into the darkness, moaning. I couldn't see him, to tell if the stuff had worked.

The doorbell rang. It was the police.

"Quick, Izzy, we've got to get that stuff into the vat," I yelled.

We dumped in the rest of the antidote. Then we walked around to the front of the house, as cool as could be.

Two police officers were peeking through the glass in the front door.

"You live here?" asked the first one.

"Yes," I said. "We just moved in."

"Well," said her partner, "We got a call saying that there was trouble here."

"Uh, trouble?" I said.

"Yes," he went on. "Something about, what was it, Margaret, an ape?"

I tried very hard to look like I didn't know what he was talking about.

"Excuse me, officers, have our sons been acting like apes again?"

It was Dad and Mom! They were back.

"Officers," said Mom, "we've just moved in

and, well, maybe we're having some small adjustment problems. But I assure you, we won't be having any more, right, Jesse?"

I nodded yes, very, very fast.

"Good," said the first officer. "Glad to hear that things are well under control. Welcome to Parkville. It's nice to have normal people living in this house again."

The officers turned and walked away.

Just then the front door opened. It was Harry, good old Harry back to normal.

"Sorry about the mess we made, Mom. It was my fault. I'm cleaning it up right now."

"Need some help, Harry?" I asked.

"Thanks, Jesse," said Harry. "I sure do."

Izzy said a quick good-bye and dashed home.

I walked in the door. Harry put his arm around my shoulders and we got right to work.

"See, Margie," said Dad. "Our boys may have their disagreements, but they always find a way to work things out."

It took all afternoon and most of the evening to clean up the big mess, not just from the clock. There were the pizza boxes, the dishes, all the stuff that we usually do at the last minute instead of battling with samurai swords and baseball bats.

I fell into bed that night as tired as I was the first night we came to Parkville. So I was really feeling goofy. I was lying on my bed, just waiting to nod out. What a weekend!

Too bad Mom and Dad would never find out. They probably wouldn't believe the story anyway. All the evidence was gone. Harry was back to normal, although I thought he was a lot hairier now than he was before. And anyway, Harry and I swore a blood oath, and I have never broken a blood oath and I never will.

I sat up in my bed. Blood oath! That meant that Harry and I had mixed our blood, while he was turning into an ape. Mr. Albert said that his formula worked through the blood! Was I going to turn into an ape?

I looked at my hands. The backs of them were covered with fine, light brown hair, much more than I ever remembered seeing before. And my feet, my feet looked more and more like monkey hands. Was I just goofy? Or was it happening to me, too?

7635098R00104

Made in the USA
San Bernardino, CA
12 January 2014